ROY BETTRIDGE

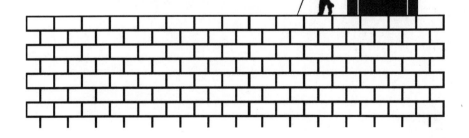

ROY BETTRIDGE

First Published 2017 by Pot Luck
Cover Design by Jamie Rae
Internal Layout and Design by Alan Hayes

A Pot Luck book

ALSO BY ROY BETTRIDGE
Look (Stop Me If You've Heard This One…) But There Was This TV Show
Flood

This book is lovingly and respectfully dedicated to;

PATRICK MACNEE
(1922 – 2015)

&

BRIAN CLEMENS
(1932 – 2015)

&

LEONARD WHITE
(1916 – 2016)

&

JON ROLLASON
(1931 – 2016)

SESSION ONE

My name is Mark Gardiner.

This feels so awkward.

Here I am, a fully grown man writing in a silly journal given to us by a counsellor trying to help me in my marriage. It's like I'm back at school, writing those bloody essays. This is all so pointless. Here I am putting my whole life and marriage troubles into a book that is going to be read by an overqualified quack (and I don't care who reads that!).

I've just had that 'married man moment'. The doctor (who will be reading this) is female, so she should understand what I mean by the 'married man moment'. Doctor Louise Foster is her name. All it means to me at the moment is that she is someone a little bit overqualified and has enough letters after her name to permit a second alphabet to be formed. I bet you would know a lot about the 'married man moment', wouldn't you, Doc? That moment where your brain keeps screaming because you know that your wife is nagging you to get back to the point of the matter when you really don't want to.

Okay, I'll start again.

My name is Mark Gardiner. I'm 36 years old and I'm being made to feel like an absolute dick, filling these pages out. What is it with these so-called doctors? They think that you can either talk or write down your problem and it all goes away.

Rubbish.

Well, I'm here in my little office, which is really my front room because my wife won't allow me to write in the bedroom. That's *her* space. I'm surrounded here by females. One is a nag and the other one claims to be a professional therapist. And as for the next stupid question on this sheet, yes, I am a married man. That is the reason I'm here after all. Can you believe it? I am a couple's therapy and marriage guidance patient and they still have to ask if I'm married. I've been married for twelve years.

My name is Jennifer Gardiner.

I'm 35 years old and I have been married to Mark for twelve years. We've been together since we were teenagers and, even though I've insisted on bringing him here, I love him to pieces. I love everything about him but it was definitely essential that we came to a couple's therapist. Things have got bad and I didn't know where to turn. I'm enjoying the fact that I can write down how I'm feeling because it comes naturally to me. With Mark, you will have your work cut out, because he's as blunt as an anvil. But to reiterate the point; we've been having some trouble and I felt that we needed help. We tried talking about it... Arguing about it would be more honest. Mark doesn't trust doctors and doesn't like the fact that doctors are what the whole point of us being here is based around. But I did insist that we needed help. We've reached a very critical stalemate and we need some guidance.

I suppose I should apologise.

Don't get me wrong, Doc, but I feel very much like an experiment that has to be watched constantly and monitored. That is what is happening to us, after all. We write in these books and you give us notes to work on. It's exactly like being at school. So, I apologise for my opening remarks.

Despite the words of derision I aimed at my wife, I do love her.

I love Jen with my whole soul.

We were in the same school together. It was senior school and I think it was year nine. The school used to have this long corridor where everyone had a locker placed. Hers was at one end of the corridor and mine was at the top of it by the hall entrance.

I asked her out on a Wednesday, not long after a PE lesson. We were putting our things away and I caught sight of her at the locker. She had a great bum, I remember thinking.

Mark has always loved my bum.

I've tailored that over the years with a good selection of underwear. But he used that to introduce himself to me. I was hanging around with a mutual friend of ours and he just came up behind me and slapped my bum. He then acted as though nothing had happened and stood there whilst the stinging on my arse slowly went away. Although I thought that I should report the incident, I didn't. He looked very cheeky but I need to be honest and admit that I really didn't fancy him at first.

I thought a slap was better than a pinch. Plus it was the only way I could think of to break the ice. I should've just said hello, but when you're thirteen you don't really know how to talk to someone. Also, if I'm being honest, I just wanted to feel her arse. But I wouldn't recommend performing the same trick to anyone. You should only do it if you think that there is a future in it and thankfully there was.

About three weeks after the slapping incident we finally got talking and we found that we were soon to have some classes together. I would always try to catch her eye and she would be rolling her eyes in disgust at me. But I pursued her and we finally became closer. We all had the old style mobile phones back then (a brick with an aerial on top) and we eventually swapped numbers after sharing a table in History class. We kind of became the school couple that everyone talked about.

He thinks we were the Royal couple at school, but we weren't.

It took a long time for the two of us to get together because I was trying my best to resist his advances. But I let my guard down a bit in the end because Mark was the only person that seemed to be chasing me. We eventually got together how teenagers do; in a very silly, over-the-top clichéd form room romance. We were never spoken about because we never became what you call a 'proper' item, we just fancied each other. Most of my friends at that time thought I was mad to be interested in him. But I saw something there. He was quite sexy at times, but they never saw that in him because, like all males, he prefers to be ruled by a false sense of macho pride. But his soft side is there.

I've got a hard man's image.

That bugs Jen a little bit, even now. I think that was the reason we drifted apart in school.

I didn't want a relationship with him at that point.

9

He was a little bit of a dick and he hung around with people who wanted to cause trouble for the teachers and moon everyone. And although I've come to appreciate my husband's arse, I didn't relish seeing his other friends shit stains every morning before lessons.

I started to really get to know Jen around year eleven, I think?

I began properly seeing Mark in year eleven.
We had all been given the choices of going to college or staying on in sixth form and we both stayed on. We then got together and I don't know what happened but I just looked at him and thought one thing and that was, "I want you".

She let me know her feelings quickly.
I had just been playing a game of football on the school playing field. It wasn't a regular school day; it was a fundraiser for local charities, where, once or twice a year, we were allowed to be in school just to chill and do what we wanted for a whole afternoon. And it was this one day, a Friday as I recall. It was a bloody hot day and half of us were stripped to the waist, including me. I thought she was looking at someone else but the whistles and cheers coming from Jen were for me I'm quite happy to say.

Somehow, Mark got fit.
He looked gorgeous and I have no idea how it happened. He went from being someone who was attractive on the eye to being an assault on all my senses and I wanted to melt a chocolate bar over him. I fancied him that much. But there was a spanner put in the works, so to speak.

My parents didn't want me to have a girlfriend.
It sounds medieval but that was how it was. My mum was okay with it but my dad wanted me to be focused on following him into the building trade. He was a little course back then in those days and he told me something I've never forgotten, "You can only lay the bricks when you've finished the blueprint". That was my father's take on life as well as sex education at that particular point, but thankfully I did not take that lesson

10

into my relationship with Jen. We discussed it and we made a mutual agreement.

We were good friends anyway so we decided to stay that way.
The fact that his dad felt I would be a distraction was quite right at that point. Mark disagrees but I know how the path would have been if he had followed his mind at that particular time.

Then, Jen moved away.

My mum was always moved around due to work.
Rather than travel from where we were living and using petrol expenses that she would never get back, she rented a small flat that was close to work. My dad made the sacrifice of staying at home and keeping the mortgage going whilst holding down his job and flitting to and from the flat that me and mum were staying in. We kept that situation going for about two or three years. But in that time, I didn't see Mark at all.

I lost contact with her.
At that time it didn't occur to me that she had disappeared out of family necessity. It was just the feeling of she was there one minute and gone the next. It was weird. And speaking for myself, I didn't keep the line of communication going very well.

Mark is crap at keeping in touch.
I'm better at contact. To this day, his parents are always shocked when they get a phone call from him because they know that he has only done so because I've reminded him to call them (laughs). I am a good daughter-in-law in that respect. But the line of communication between us was a little bit non-existent at that point because we both didn't really know where to begin.

I did miss Jen, a lot.
I fancied her like hell and it looked like I had lost her.

I did miss Mark.

We were just starting to get close and the fact that I had to pull away did a small amount of damage. I was optimistic that I would see him again and, as I've told him, if he had stayed in touch at that point then things may have been different. But we didn't see each other or contact each other so we both went in the directions we were guided into.

I knuckled down into my dad's business.

He was a licensed building contractor who had built the business up from scratch. He would always tell us about how proud he was to have everything in the house earned by the sweat and tears that he had laboured over every day. He thought that I had the brains to follow him into the trade. He sent me off to business school so that I could learn the ins and outs of a spreadsheet and keep the books in the black rather than the red. He would religiously go through blueprints and tell me how important planning was in the early stages of building. Although I did follow in dad's footsteps, after three years of education and over two years of training at his side, we had a fallout that lasted for a couple of months. I wanted to use all the knowledge that I had got from learning about the business to go out on my own, rather than work for my dad. He was angry because he wanted me to be rigid and learn fully under his wing. He didn't trust me to do it at the end of the day.

So I looked into starting up on my own. I borrowed some money from the bank and started out as a private hire, rather than announce myself in the trade columns. I'm a card player when I get the chance for a game, so I called the company Full Deck, a name that my father later congratulated me for coming up with, as he thought it was catchy.

I went to college.

In the beginning, I was unsure of what avenue to take because I have very domineering parents and the only reason that they sent me off to college was to try and find something that was going to be lucrative, so I didn't come back to them with cap in hand wanting money. I sadly fell into the trap of being involved with numbers. I was always told that I had a head for figures and my numeracy level at school was always top of the class. But the jobs were pretty low on the ground to start with. I spent a few years behind the tills at a stationery seller. I then went into working at a burger joint for a couple of months before I entertained the idea of signing on. Then I hit a break after three days of searching for something with numbers. I got an odd job at a surveyors and one of the clients we had was an accountant looking at branching out his offices. I was assigned to look after the project and handle all the forms and paperwork. Soon after that I got a letter from the accountant saying that there was a vacancy in his firm as his right hand.

I asked my mum and dad what they thought and they advised me to go for it. So I went there on a trial period that became extended pretty quickly and I was there for a good number of years.

I wondered if I would see Jen again.

I had something to prove to her and it was that I had not become a waster. I had done something with my life when everyone was worrying if I would ever get there. I suppose I wanted to show off. But we're all a bit like that, aren't we, Doc? We all like to be noticed and given the credit for the things we do and I was very proud that I had got somewhere in life. I wanted to share it with someone, and that someone was Jen. How we got back in touch was a complete surprise.

The reunion with Mark was special.

The office we had needed some building work doing on it and I thought it would be cost efficient to have an independent builder or contractor, because you can then simply set your bid for their services and they can either say yes or no. So, after I was given the green light for the idea, I looked around for the contractor.

The company we used was called Full Deck and had the logo of a pack of playing cards with a wrecking ball on it. And much to my surprise, I rang the company and found that I was dealing with Mark on the other end of the line.

She needed a builder to do some work on the office and I was all for it.

The estimate was cheap, but my mind wasn't on the work at that point. It was focused on the lady on the other end of the line.

I met up with Mark to discuss the work that needed doing at the office.

I hadn't seen him for a fair number of years, so I was a little nervous. He was early to the appointment, I remember. And he had styled his hair with gel for some strange reason. But he was wearing a nice shirt and he had clearly come to the meeting prepared to do business.

I got there early to impress Jen.

I tried my hardest to be the opposite of how she would remember me. If I had been late then she would have thought that nothing had changed with me and that nothing could happen between us, so I wanted to prove that things had changed.

She arrived in her business outfit. My god, she looked gorgeous.

He had got more buff over the years.

I sat opposite him and we discussed the possibility of business. But from that moment I quite honestly would have straddled him if the restaurant wasn't crowded. I was hot for him, okay!

She was all about business at that meeting.

We discussed the whole project and set out when my lot could start the work at her office. But I didn't want to leave it at that, so I plucked up the courage to do something about it.

Mark openly said that he wanted to see me again.

He pointed out that the number on his business card was also his private line and that I should give him a call. My husband can be a smooth talker when he wants to be!

She eventually rang.

I held onto Mark's card for ages because I was nervous. I didn't keep him waiting intentionally, but I kept either putting the card into my desk and forgetting to take it home with me or staring at it for hours, going to call him and then chickening out at the last moment.

14

The phone then went and it was like an angel talking down the phone.

I rang.
I wasn't sure what to talk about and he barely said a word during that initial call. We covered all the past and did the usual thing you do when you catch up with someone that you used to know. It surprised me at just how far he had come in all those years. I had a high opinion of him but I think he felt that I had a low opinion of him, which I have never understood. So we chatted for over an hour and he then asked me to dinner.

I felt that I needed to wine and dine Jen.

It had been a long time and I wanted to make the best impression that I could. So I rang a mate who worked in a restaurant and asked him if he could get me the best table in the place.

Mark was specific in his requirements for me.
We had dated a little in our school time together and one evening we went to a school get-together that they had copied from the American teen shows that do so well over here. And on that particular night I wore a dress and he was smitten with the idea of me in a dress.

I told her, "Put on the best dress that you have…"

And when I got to the restaurant I must've been there for a good twenty minutes or so before she arrived. I was so nervous and I must've drunk six or seven glasses of water. It wasn't long before I was winning the award for best and longest at peeing in a restaurant toilet, but thankfully I got all of that out of the way before she arrived.

On our first proper date I was running late.
I went through my whole wardrobe looking for this best dress that he wanted to see me in. In all honesty, I didn't care about business. I just wanted to see him. He'd already set my senses going and I didn't want to blow any chances I had to do the same to him. So, after hours of searching, I finally found what I was looking for and what he wanted. It was a backless dress so I didn't think that it would fail on any level.

Jen then entered the restaurant.

As she walked to my table, she proved to me that she was the sexiest woman I had ever seen in my life.

I walked in and I saw Mark's eyes pop out of his head like champagne corks.

The dinner was great and he actually did order some champagne for us. He was really quite a gentleman with everything.

I went the whole hog.

I didn't give a shit about the cost. Jen is worth every pound I have and still is.

I then thought he was taking me home, but he led me in a different direction.

I felt that I had lost time to make up.

So I booked us into a hotel.

He paid for two separate rooms next to each other.

I asked Mark why he had done this. He said, "I want the first person I see in the morning to be you." But I then pointed out that we were not staying in the same room. Quick as a flash he said, "That's why I'm treating you to breakfast".

He had won me over anyway by not seizing the opportunity to bed me straight away; that made me fancy him even more.

Breakfast the next morning allowed me to get to know her properly and by that I mean we could go away from the pretences of business and just be ourselves.

At the breakfast we reconnected completely. We covered everything that we wanted to cover; we chatted endlessly about likes and dislikes, and we wanted to know if we still had anything in common. It was absolute bliss because it was as though we were ticking every box and starting afresh.

I asked Jen for another date right then.

I didn't want to lose her again and felt that I needed to make a bit more effort than I had done before. In all fairness to myself, I think I was definitely ahead on points with what I had done the night before.

Mark pulled out the stops.

He was completely open and I was struck by that. He wasn't pouring his heart out but he was letting me know that there was still something there. And I think that he could sense that I was feeling the same way about it. We arranged a third date after the second one.

By the third date I was so in love with her.

I had already made up my mind to do something about it during our second date but I held back a little bit on it. I didn't want to appear to be too eager. Plus, I didn't want to overtly rush her into anything. I really didn't know how she felt towards me at the time. Jen thinks that I did but in truth I really, honestly, had no idea if she had any feelings towards me in any way.

Mark was such a gentleman.

He was picking me up, taking me out, bringing me home, and buying me flowers. He was being a little bit mushy, but I wasn't complaining. But he then shocked me.

I proposed to Jen after finishing our third date and I dropped her back at her place.

We had been to see a movie.

Mark will remember this differently but this is what happened.

He picked me up and decided that he would take me to the cinema. We were halfway there when he turned the car round and took me back home. I wondered what the hell was going on and he just sat there in silence.

He then turned to me and just said, 'Will you marry me?'

I said yes immediately. I knew that I had feelings for him and they were already developing into something a lot more meaningful. Plus I wanted him and I wasn't going to hide that any more. And the minute I said yes to him, it led to bed.

Jen has a body that is worth waiting for.
I just couldn't wait any longer.

We got physical a lot after he proposed.
It was like someone had opened the bottle of pop and let the air out. He was definitely worth the wait. And I was very surprised that he waited so long. I thought that the first thing he would have done was to try and undress me at our first date. So I was quite happy with my choice of partner and the fact he was a good boy!

I let Jen organise the wedding.
I already got what I wanted from the day and that was her.

Mark agreed to take a back seat with us getting married.
He said to me, "This is your day. Do things how you want them…"
And I've done that ever since we married!

We didn't tell anybody.

We wanted our wedding kept quiet.
Both our parents didn't think highly of our choice of partner and he knew that I didn't want that to ruin the whole thing. So we told a few friends and got married in the local registry office.

Jen was the sexiest bride you would ever see in your life.
I saw her walk down the aisle and thought to myself, "You've hit the jackpot, son!"

He was getting frisky during the vows!
He was pulling me close to him and the minute that the pictures were being taken in the gardens outside, I could feel his hand on my bum so he was definitely feeling fresh!

18

I don't think she was wearing underwear that day.

I wore a thong at the wedding especially for Mark.
I knew what he would be like!

Jen has got sexier to me since we married.

I don't know where things started to go a little wrong, but my feelings about her haven't changed. I have the sexiest wife in the world. I love her to death.

I'm so lucky to have Mark.
I love him with all my heart. But things have been testing us recently and have led us to this point. And I don't feel a distance from him but his actions have put a bit of a wedge there. And it's not his fault, I know that.

Well I've finally said it, Doc! I love Jennifer. I love her. I LOVE her!

Bet you're happy you've had a breakthrough!

Sorry, I don't mean to be sarcastic. It's just remembering everything up to this point is getting to me. You try and find where things have gone wrong but you're not quite sure if anything has gone wrong. I still can't get to grips with why we're here in therapy. I suppose things unravelled after Jen and I moved into the house.

Mark had got this beautiful house through a contact in the business.
We had been married for about a month and we weren't even properly living together, work that one out! We were staying in a two bed flat that was mouldy, damp and near rat infested. It was horrible and we had been cheated on the purchase due to the surveyor getting his own back against the company I used to work for.

It turned out that the provider of the property had got into a problem with the surveying company. He then did a background check on Jen and found the name of the surveyor she used to work for and used that as a revenge tactic in the hope that she would go back to them and cause a scene.

It was all very childish and we were in the middle of it.

So I asked a few friends if they had specially built houses going in the area because I was getting married and wanted a decent place to live.

We moved into the house on our third month of being married and it wasn't an immediate struggle to begin with.

The fact of my business being independent means you rely on the amount of money that is put down on the contract. I was doing okay but I think the worry of it set in with Jen at the beginning.

He was a busy man.
But there was a feeling every month; was he going to be busy for three weeks or three months? And I had never been in that situation before. It scared me but I trusted my husband to see things were okay.

Jen got the flat cleared out pretty quickly.

Mark's crap was all that was there in reality.
There were endless boxes that covered the whole flat and I asked my sister to help me shift it up to the house. My stuff was okay but I wanted all things to be new.

We argued about the amount of stuff that I had.

There were VHS tapes that I refused to get rid of, cassettes that I wanted to keep, stereos that had seen better days. They were minor disagreements but she hated the fact that I was a pack rat!

Mark, get all your shit out of my house!
That is basically what I would say to him.

I would spend hours going through what I had managed to keep hold of. Jen would wonder when I was going to come to bed because I went through every VHS tape to check that they were okay.

20

The flat he had kept all of this in was very damp and he wanted to make sure that every tape was in good working order (sighs) get with the 21st century and upgrade to Blu-ray for god sake!

Jen did get annoyed over one tape.

He would play one tape with the volume full blast.
It was a show called The Avengers and I never got why he played it so loudly. He told me that the sound wasn't very good. Sounded bloody excellent from upstairs!

The Avengers wasn't my tape.
It was one I found in the flat when we moved into it. I just acquired it and liked what I saw. It was a weird programme that seemed to make a sort of sense as you followed it. A bit like that other weird show, *The Prisoner*. Plus *The Avengers* has spies in it, so I fell in love it.

I did try to change his collections over the time.
I said to him, "Babe, the James Bond films you taped from ITV are available on DVD. You'll see the difference because there's no advert breaks on them!"

Jen is quite sarcastic over my stuff.

The first major change with Mark occurred when he got more business.

The contracts were coming at me thick and fast.
Both Jen and I did not see something like this happening and as it was my company I took a firm hold in the way things were done.

We had to schedule everything nearly.

Sex was never timetabled.
I would shag Jen on the job site and she knew it!

21

As forthcoming as Mark was, I did not want to make love on a pile of bricks!
Our bed is there for a reason!

We spent our first Christmas as a married couple not seeing each other!

With my office commitments and Mark working so hard at the job site, we had no time together. We hated it but we couldn't argue at the money that it was bringing in for us. We both understood it and that was that.

Even at New Year we were both working. But I blame myself for that one.

Mark does beat himself up a bit, bless him.
I've never knocked the way he works and he's a hard worker. It's just we never got to meet in the middle at the beginning of things. It was tough for me and it was tough for him. But things then changed again.

I got a contract thrust under my nose for a possible extension being granted to the Leisure Centre that wasn't far from where we lived. It was a large amount of money, not enough for Jen and I to retire on but it was good money.

He showed me the numbers and I nearly fainted.

I went ahead in getting a crew together and signed a deal to get the scaffolding up and get the blueprints issued. I even asked Jen what she thought about the design because that, in many respects, was our time together.

He wanted me to join him on the job site while he worked on this extension. And I went for about four days and I got to see how my husband worked. It was quite fun and we actually got to spend some time together.

She did enjoy embarrassing me in front of the guys, too!

I would make Mark kiss me before he went off to do any work. And then when everyone was having a break, I would tell dirty jokes as everyone was eating.

Jen knows more dirty jokes than I do. She could easily be one of the guys if she wanted. It made me fancy her even more, if I'm honest. My wife the bloke!

The building work then got under way and I left him to it.

Jen went back to her world of numbers and I got back to my world of building.

He was about two weeks into the building of it when it happened.

Jen would be better at the dates of it.
What happened was the deadline for the construction to be finished was upped by the powers that be and that left us with not enough time or manpower to finish it. It was in the middle of winter as well, so it was freezing cold and half of my guys were going down with colds and flu.

Mark was working round the clock.
He was doing the job of about three people and it showed when he would get home completely exhausted. But then they hit a snag when they found that they were going to have to get out some heavy machinery on the site to bring the deadline in on time.

We got the demolition crew in.
I was working round the clock. I was starting at five in the morning, getting home to Jen at six in the evening and was in bed by eight every night. It was a hard slog and the first week was us getting to grips with how we were going to tackle the project. And the next week was the fatal week.

It happened on the Saturday.
I had arranged to spend some time with Mark and had made plans.

23

I was on the site for a couple of hours that morning.

I wanted to oversee that all was in place for the day's work and that everyone could manage.

What Mark didn't know was the guy in charge of the wrecking ball was a rookie who had only been shown how to work it rather than practically be tested on it.

This guy told me that he had handled the ball before.

He seemed quite genuine about it and spoke like he knew his stuff. I then went to one of the portaloos that was on the site for us. I was sat on the loo doing what comes naturally. And whatever happened next, I don't remember.

The wrecking ball hit the portaloo that Mark was in and sent him flying over to the other side of the field. I was waiting for him to come home and he was about an hour or so late, which wasn't like him. The phone then rang and I was told that he had been rushed to hospital.

I woke up in an ambulance with people staring at me; everyone on the site was looking through the back of the ambulance doors sniggering because I still had my trousers round my ankles. And the thing that worried me most was whether I had tissue stuck on my arse. That was the only thing I was worried about!

I got to the hospital and they were still doing tests on him when I got there.

He was wired up to every machine imaginable. There were doctors coming in every ten minutes and nurses were checking him over. At one point I couldn't get near the bed to see him because he was being examined so thoroughly.

Jen looked worried as hell.

She had to stand there whilst I was being prodded and looked at by all these doctors. They did the sight test on me to check if I had blurred vision. They had painkillers on standby in case I got any sort of a headache.

It was worrying to see him like that.

I don't like hospitals much and Jen knew I didn't.
I wanted out of there. I didn't want to be looked at any more.

He wasn't the easiest patient but he listened to me when I told him it was for his own good

I was in there for about two days.
Jen stayed in the hospital with me and I insisted that she share the bed with me.

Do you really think that being in hospital would cure my husband's appetites?
He wanted to get frisky in hospital so that proved to me that he was ready to come home!

I have a very sexy wife. You can't blame me for trying!

We were told by the doctor that if he had any sudden changes in mood or anything along those lines to let them know immediately.

I was told that I might have a delayed concussion.
I was also told not to go back to work for a few weeks so everything had to be overseen by my right hand man whilst I was at home.

When he got home after the accident, Mark entered a very slow progression into what I deemed weird behaviour, things that were not really him.

I was occupying my time with television.
I was watching a lot of sports so I kept up to date with games and everything else which I was happy about.

The only thing that didn't change was him shouting at the telly when his team didn't score a goal! So, at the start, it was all nice and rosy.

Jen and I kind of reconnected a little at that point.

It was nice having him at home.
I got to see him off duty for a few days rather than a few hours. We had fallen into that rut of getting used to only seeing each other during working hours and I don't think we knew how to pull back from it. It's very easy to fall into that rut but you then run the risk of resenting the time that your partner actually wants to spend with you when you have the time spare. We initially avoided feeling that way about each other. But having him home was a good thing.

I got through the rest of everything that I had moved up from the flat.
Jen tells me that the problem began from there, but I really can't remember how or what happened.

Mark had free time and I suggested that he go through all of the boxes of tapes that he had brought up from the flat. I didn't look into anything along the lines of storage because I wasn't sure that we had the space for it.

I reached an agreement with Jen that we keep out what I would frequently watch and place the rest into the loft.

But I didn't want him struggling to get into the loft so soon after the incident at work. So I went up and put away anything that he didn't want in plain sight so it was out of the way and the agreement made could be stuck to.

Then one evening, Jen went out.

I went to visit my mum and Mark was left to his own devices at home. He knew there was a tape in the machine already because it was the only one that he hadn't said anything about to me, so I left him to it.

The tape was *The Avengers* and I remember that it captured my attention.

I must have been out for a few hours and I came back to Mark sat staring at the telly watching this tape in the machine. I thought he would be watching the sports channel as usual but he surprised me by watching The Avengers. Mainly because he was watching an episode that was in black and white, which he's not keen on.

I don't normally watch black and white. I find it dull and I can't normally get my head around anything in it. It doesn't hold me. I wasn't brought up on anything black and white because I could never fully interact with it. I used to make my dad angry whenever he would try and watch a black and white movie that was repeated on the TV because I would talk all the way through it.

He still doesn't believe me when I tell him that his eyes were glued to the screen.

Jen has always said that my attention was unbreakable during a part of the show that was in black and white. I struggle to believe that but I know she wouldn't lie to me, so it must've been true.

He was watching it. He was happy. So, I left him to it.

I then apparently became a bit unsociable.

Mark didn't want to go out.
He wouldn't explain the reason why and I got fed up of asking him. He just didn't want to leave the house. I put it down to a security kind of thing. It wasn't long after the accident and the doctors had warned me that he may cling onto things that he found familiar or that he felt were something of a security blanket for him.

I didn't want to miss anything on the telly!

It did lead to one showdown of sorts.

27

I came down and found him asleep in the chair whilst the channel was on Babestation. I wasn't happy about that.

I was watching something else and fell asleep. I didn't choose the Babestation channel. At least I don't remember choosing the channel. I'm lying, Doc…

I then insisted that he come to bed at the same time as I did after the Babestation incident. I let my anger go because I didn't want to fall out over an insecurity.
But he couldn't switch off.

I would lay there next to Jen and stare at the ceiling.

I'm writing this now and can't believe that I am forming that sentence. But I would be lying next to my very gorgeous and sexy wife and doing nothing about it! And the strange factor is that as she was there snoring away like a trouper, not once did it cross my mind to wake her up and say, "Babe, do you fancy a shag?" How stupid is that?

I asked if sleeping tablets might help him but he was unsure.

I wasn't on any medication from doctors, but I didn't feel as though I needed help sleeping. I just couldn't sleep. My brain wouldn't switch off and when it did switch off it only felt like I had been asleep for a few minutes because the alarm clock would go off. It was nuts.

This went on for about three weeks.
He was napping at certain points during the day. I didn't think there was anything wrong with it but it might have been altering any sort of pattern that he used to have. We even tried watching television in bed together but all that would do was cause more arguments because he would watch programmes nearly all through the night.

Jen was trying everything in the book to try and sort this out.

I tried to keep him awake during the day.
I tried making him do several things around the house at one time, washing the car, cooking dinner for us on certain nights. The overall aim was to make him tired so he could get a decent night sleep.

She even got spicy in bed, which she then informed me I didn't rise to.

Knowing me in the brief passages that you have read, Doc, you will know that I find my wife to be the sexiest woman ever. Believe me when I say that I do not like admitting that the sexiest woman in the world could not work her magic on me.

I bought a new nightdress.
It was a backless silk number and thought that if the day had been a failure in getting him tired then there was nothing wrong in being physical.

That didn't go down well, with both of us. I still feel a little bitter about it now.

For me, I have the hottest wife on the planet. Due to this accident I wasn't able to act on instincts anymore. My eyes were fine but they were not connecting with the rest of my body because seeing my wife in that nightdress was somehow not causing my heart to beat out of my chest.

Nothing happened, which wasn't like Mark.
All I would have to do with him was wink and he was in the mood for sex. But this time around, it was frightening. This had never happened before and I immediately thought that he had gone off me and wasn't interested any more.

Jen is the sexiest woman I've ever known.

Nothing in the world would stop me being interested in her. But at that point, I did think that there was something wrong and I told her so.

I went back to the doctor with him.
We were told that there was nothing to worry about and that his body was probably dealing with the shock of the incident that had happened to him. I wasn't so sure about the diagnosis but I went along with it.

29

Jen has got really good instincts.

After we came home from the appointment she told me that she didn't fully believe in the doctor's words. At first I thought that she was just being silly because, in all honesty, I had no idea of what was fully happening. It sounds unusual but that is how it felt at the time. Jen insisted that the doctor could be wrong. But there wasn't really much more that we could do.

I rang the hospital.

I wanted to speak to the consultant that we had seen and I told him about Mark's changes in behaviour. The sleepless nights and lack of intimacy didn't surprise him but I was told to be patient and keep an eye on him. So that's what I did.

Things then went back to a sort of normality.

The late nights slowly became normal.

Mark would come to bed, but he would be doing so at two or three in the morning. I would hear an assortment of shows from downstairs. They were all mainly sports related. But I did notice that he was watching the same tape more than once and that tape was The Avengers.

I don't remember being fixated on one thing but Jen told me that I was.

I suppose I should've said something or done something about it but I didn't. I wish that I had, otherwise we wouldn't be in this current situation.

We then started to fight more.

I was trying to snap him out of it.

The only way that I thought that I could get the best reaction was by arguing and I was picking fights about the smallest things to try and re-awaken his interest in life outside of the television.

One fight which I do remember happened just after my birthday.

I made dinner for us and then Mark went back to the television.
The Avengers was blaring away. It was a colour episode this time and I
had heard the theme tune so much that I was singing it to myself at times; it
was odd and at times irritating. But I knew that I had to cut him off from it,
literally. So, midway through whatever he was watching I came in from the
kitchen and stood directly in front of the TV screen.

She screamed at me.

I went for it like I never had before. I then unplugged the television and
threw the plug at him. I called him uncaring and inconsiderate along with
everything else under the sun.

I tried to fight back but didn't get very far.

He seemed to be struggling for a comeback. I think it was because he knew
I was right. I'm always right where he's concerned!

The problem then disappeared because as Jen was stood there raging at
me all I was thinking about taking her to the bedroom.

He got horny within five minutes of me screaming at him.

I won't bug you with the rest, Doc!

It was the most interesting attempt at sex that we had because it didn't last
long.
We got into it and started fumbling around and the next thing I remember
is hearing snoring as his head just passed my boobs. So the biggest plus of that
evening was that I managed to get to sleep without hearing the television on all
night.

Falling asleep just as you're about to have sex? I think that it's another fight waiting to happen!

Strangely enough, I wasn't angry at the time.
I sympathised with him and just let him rest because I think he needed to have some form of a release and be familiar with what he used to do prior to being chucked halfway across a building site.

I was fine for the next few weeks.

He returned to normal for about two weeks.
We got back to being a couple again and it was really nice. He would do sweet things like breakfast in bed and do all the housework for me. If I had been to work all day he would go out and buy some flowers and have them waiting for me on the table when I got in. It was lovely. It was like living a dream.

Jen is the greatest woman in the world.

I would do anything for her and I'm not above doing my fair share of anything. She does it for me so I would always repay that. But sometimes there are things that happen just around the corner.

He then insisted on a clear out.

I saw that we could hardly move around the house because of all these boxes that we had brought up from the flat. So I said to Jen, "Let's put them away."

Everything that he had gone through was then put into the loft.
The only thing left out was the Avengers tape.

I don't know how I overlooked the *Avengers* tape, but it wasn't a big deal.

Soon after that, Mark started acting funny again.

I don't remember what happened at the time, but Jen has told me about this only recently.

Apparently I was doing things that were embarrassing.

He started to carry an umbrella everywhere with him.

It could be a warm sunny day and there he would be with an umbrella. He wouldn't let it go. If he was around the house, he would twirl it in his hand. It was ridiculous and there were a few times that it caused trouble. The most memorable one was when he was making a cup of coffee. He broke three mugs because he was twirling the umbrella at the same time he was putting the ingredients in. And there was another time that he was just walking around the room and I was coming up behind him to go into the kitchen. He twirled the umbrella and nearly caught me with the tip of it. No matter how angry I got with him about it, he did not seem fazed at all.

Whatever she tells you, Doc, I have no memory of it.

I then invited some friends for dinner.

Mark came downstairs in a clean and pressed white shirt, his best trousers, his best polished shoes and he was wearing a bow tie. The rest of us were in jeans, trainers and casual clothing and my husband was done up like a penguin. We all just laughed it off at the time but then someone had the bright idea for us to go bowling.

How do you explain to complete strangers and the succession of laughing kids in the building that the man you have walked into a crowded bowling alley with, and who is the only person dressed up as though he's meeting the Queen, is your husband?

I wanted the ground to eat me whole. It was so embarrassing. And he did not look in the slightest bit concerned. He even caught sight of himself in the reflection of the mirror behind the drinks bar and didn't even flinch. In his head he looked normal. The rest of us were trying our best to get on with the game and I just wanted to get out of there. We got home and I didn't speak to him for the rest of the night.

There was a weekend where we had another fight.

33

My mum visited us.

She had known about Mark's accident and was concerned about how we were doing. And he kept referring to her as Mrs Riley. He had always called her mum since we got married and although she wasn't fond of him as a son-in-law at first she liked that he called her mum. It made her warm to him. But he kept calling her Mrs Riley.

The fact that my mum's name was Murray had completely left his mind. At that moment I was wondering if he had a mind at all.

There was something that happened with Jen's dad as well.

My dad always liked Mark.

He was the one in my family who was always on my side if I ever wanted to see Mark and he would always do battle with my mother about it. He would've walked me down the aisle at our wedding but my mother was not going to allow anything like that at that particular time. And dad saw Mark's behaviour and became quite concerned. He took me to one side and actually admitted to me that he was worried about him. For my dad to say that about someone told me that it was serious. Now, dad would always take Mark for a drink whenever he visited, because he liked the fact that they bonded so well. And they came back from the pub and dad was looking a little off colour. I asked him what the problem was and he said that Mark had been talking as though he thought he was a character from Mission: Impossible.

Jen told me this and I couldn't help but laugh.

If I was not in this situation and had to be writing these pointless notes for you, Doc, then I wouldn't believe a word of it. I'm not calling my wife a liar, but it did seem a little far-fetched, even for me. And apparently it didn't stop there…

Mark had taken my dad into the beer garden at the pub and told him that there was a particular group of people that he had been watching for some time in our garden shed. And my dad, being who he is, went along with it.

As I've been told (I still don't believe it) we both made a scene for Jen and her mum.

I then watched the second part of this drama happen.
My dad and my husband came home and then started going around the garden looking for invisible people. My mum thought that it was a laugh and my dad thought he was a kid again. But they didn't know that Mark was being deadly serious.

Before you ask, Doc, I do not believe in invisible people.

It scared me.
I then began to think that Mark had been seriously damaged by that wrecking ball.

Things then settled again.

Mark then went back to normal again.
I was so unsure of how this was going to go. I was wondering whether I should call the doctors or just let it carry on until it stopped naturally. I just didn't know what to do. But the first choice that I made was to get him out of the house because he had lapsed back to just sitting in front of the TV.

Jen pushed me about a bit!

I had to get him out of the house.
He hadn't engaged with reality for a while and I felt that he needed to. His behaviour was questionable but at that point it was easy to deal with.

She got me seeing friends that I hadn't seen for a while. She even suggested that some of the guys from the job site take me back to work for a bit to see how things were going.

I think it was the right thing to do.

35

His mind wasn't being fully occupied and I didn't want to be married to a couch potato. So I rang up Jamie, a good friend of Mark's and the second-in-command on the site while he was away. I suggested that maybe just a few hours a day would be good to ease him back into a routine.

It was good to be back there.

I got all the jokes thrown at me because of the incident in the portaloo; "Duck everyone! Mark's having a shit and it's gonna knock you out!!"

He came home happy, that was the main thing.

My husband was still there. I hadn't fully lost him and I was very happy about that.

Going back to work full time was next on the agenda.

Jen had told me that because I had been going to the site for a couple of hours a day each week, it was something of a preparation period for going back into work completely. I didn't argue with her. If anything, I was all up for going back to the job site.

He had been at home for the amount of time the doctors had told him to take off.

Looking back on it now I think that selfishness was the key to me making him go back. He probably wasn't ready but I didn't want him being a slob and staying around the house all day. I wish that I had stopped him.

I was having a great time being back among the guys on the site.

He actually was supposed to go back to the consultant and be medically checked over before he went back full-time, but Mark was having none of it.

I didn't want to be poked and prodded again by every single person in a blue outfit and claiming to know everything in a medical dictionary. I wanted to go back to work and I genuinely thought that I had been away for a decent length of time.

I did consider ringing the doctor to be on the safe side, but we had already argued about the whole thing so much that I didn't bother. I decided to let the whole thing fall flat on its head or rise and disappear into the clouds. I just didn't realise the damage that was being done in the meantime because Mark was not well enough to go back, even though on the outside he looked it.

I got back into the routine of work slowly. I didn't go the full hog with the hours on the site because Jen didn't want me to do that.

I got a phone call from Ronnie, one of Mark's mates on the site. He told me that Mark was behaving oddly.

I would get home sometimes to face a third degree interrogation.

I confronted Mark each time about the stories I had been told.

I never took it up with the guys that kept calling the house. I just thought it was because they fancied Jen and knew she was alone!

I would be getting three to four calls a day telling me that Mark was going around the site, spouting off the top of his head about some made up crap that didn't make sense. My first thought was that he had been drinking, but he would never do something like that.

We would have constant arguments the minute that I got in the door.

I wasn't fair to Mark, I know that now.
But at that point, I was being told one thing and he was telling me another, so I didn't know what to believe.

It then came to another incident that I have no memory of again.

DOCTOR'S NOTE:
"Upon reading these journals so far, I can see clearly why this matter has been brought to my attention. I

find Mark at times a little reluctant to take this seriously, but the point of these journals is for me to assess the needs of you both as a couple. This case was referred to me personally due to the case surrounding Mark's accident and (apart from minor lapses with his aftercare) it also appears that we have only just scratched the surface and are unravelling the reasons for your visits here.

For the next session, please go into detail as it may allow Mark to loosen up and it may jog him into remembering these dark gaps in his memory. Let's begin with the incident that Mark has alluded to..."

SESSION TWO

We were out shopping.

We had been there for about ten minutes and then something just clicked inside Mark that made him go on autopilot. We were waiting at the self checkout and he turned to me and began talking to me about something called The Nutshell.

DOCTOR'S NOTE:
"For the sake of this report and the research that has been done into this particular client's history, I will denote the information referred to in the notes with the relevant background information that I have sourced for the purpose of further investigation and for the case notes reference material."

The Avengers – THE NUTSHELL (1963)
"A secret file codenamed Big Ben has been stolen from an underground base called The Nutshell. And it appears that Steed is that traitor..."

I had just put the stuff through the barcode reader and Mark started treating it as though it was reading his finger prints. The shop staff thought it was hilarious, particularly the woman at the checkout. It was alright for them. They had no idea what was really going on. He then took me over to the other side of the shop, practically dragging me. And he then stood there looking at the woman on the counter. This particular shop worker did not know what had been going on and was completely taken back by Mark's behaviour. All he kept asking her to do was to take us to a man called Disco.

I have no memory of it happening.

The manager was about to be called, but I had to tell everyone not to do anything. Just let it carry on and he will break out of it. Mark then dragged me around the different parts of the store telling me about how he had just left the escape artist that he hired to steal a file called Big Ben and clarified to me that it was not the clock in parliament square.

I'm standing there and watching while my husband is acting out this little drama in front of a very embarrassed audience. I knew how they felt because I wanted the ground to swallow me up. He was going up to people and acting out this weird scene. He gave one of the men in the crowd the name Vienna or something similar and called him the traitor. The security guard must have thought that Mark was a lunatic!

I seriously don't know what happened.

Jen thinks that I do know but I have no memory of anything that she will tell you.

He then started acting as though he had been captured by the powers that be and we finally managed to get the shopping to the car. As I drove us home, he was sitting in the car as though he was in a trance. There was nothing in his eyes and he just kept looking at the road ahead as though his life depended on it. When we got home he finally snapped out of it.

I remember Jen screaming at me.

I wanted to kill him.

The embarrassment that he made me feel in that supermarket was horrific. I couldn't go back there for six months.

I was put on the sofa for six nights.

Looking back, I know I was harsh towards Mark. Understanding was what was needed, but at the time anything containing reason just flies out of the window, doesn't it? Here I was on a simple shopping trip and my husband was dancing around the aisles as though acting out a spy movie.

Yes, I should've tried to be more understanding, but at the time I was livid.
I couldn't look at him.

I just went along with it.

My wife didn't want to be near me and it was my fault, even if I couldn't remember what I had done. She eventually talked to me and told me the whole thing, but I had no memory of doing what she described. I thought that I was going mad because it's not normal behaviour. You think to yourself that you should remember things like this and I desperately tried to remember if I had done what Jen said. I didn't go back to the supermarket and ask anybody because I felt that if I did I would be escorted from there wearing a straitjacket or led away in handcuffs. It would worry me even more that the fog wasn't beginning to clear. I did think of going to the doctor about it but chickened out in case he looked at me as though I really was a lunatic.

I was by now seriously worried about Mark.
I watched his behaviour more closely from that point on. I was concerned that further, similar incidents might follow, because if this had happened once then it could easily re-occur. I was also anxious that I might not be there when these behavioural lightning strikes hit, so I had to take appropriate action.

I went to work one morning and Jen had phoned the site.

She told everyone to keep an eye on me. I didn't like that because I felt as though I was being babysat by the people that I work with. There is no coming back from something like that because it wounds your ego and it makes you look different in their eyes. These are the people that you can really loosen up with and be a guy around. Now, they look at you as though you're a hospital case because your wife has told them to keep a special eye on you.

I did it for his own good.

That caused a few fights between us.

41

I thought that he was ill.

No person just has an episode like that and comes out of it with no memory that they have just acted the fool to an unwitting audience, not unless there was something very wrong. In hindight, I should've consulted the doctors about it, but at the time I thought that my way was the best.

And then it happened again, according to Jen.

I got a call from Mark's site foreman, Robbie. I only shared my concerns with a few of the lads down at the yard because essentially Mark was their boss. In the world of the builder it takes only one problem to cause a domino effect and have a worker considered incompetent, so I tried my best to make only the smallest group of people aware of Mark's troubles, and then only those who were close to him. As I said, I received the phone call. Robbie said that during their lunch break Mark had behaved in almost exactly the same way as in the supermarket (I had described the incident to him previously).

I have no memory of it or the details. Again, Jen might be able to fill in any gaps for you, Doc, because I certainly cannot.

I was told that some of the guys liked to go for a pub lunch and Mark tagged along. He ordered a drink and a sandwich and kept calling the landlord Piggy Warner, or something like that. To make matters worse, Mark was apparently searching for someone that he arrived with at the pub but who had since gone missing.

DOCTOR'S NOTE:
The Avengers – THE TOWN OF NO RETURN (1965)
"Searching for a missing agent, Steed and Emma Peel stumble into a town that is full of enemy agents who do not take well to uninvited guests…"

Then when he got back to the site, he started to talk to people as though they were the villains in a spy drama. He called one of his workers a vicar and apparently he was one of the team that had kidnapped his partner, who was incidentally called Jennifer. And then I was told that he started a play fight with one of them.

Part of it involved a fight with one of my workers on the site. That part of the story I can't believe. Most of them are built like brick shithouses, so if I wanted to take them on, I better have had a very good reason for doing so. Honestly, Doc, I don't believe that I started a fight with any single one of my workers on the site.

It was with his mate, Jamie, who was also his second-in-command while he was off on the sick. Apparently, they were going around the site rolling around on the ground like a couple of kids in a playground scuffle.

I know me and Jamie play around, but from what Jen told me, I can't believe that it went that far. The closest we ever get to a fight is when it's his turn to buy a round at the pub and he's being too stingy to dip his hand into his bloody pocket.

Jamie told me that it was only over when he pretended to play dead on the ground. But that was only after Mark threw him over his shoulder. I first laughed at that part of the story because Mark is a little broad but he didn't have the power to shoulder throw anybody. But Jamie insisted that this was the case.

Shoulder throw? No way. I didn't do that.

The whole thing rang in my ears just like the supermarket incident. I asked Mark about it when he got home from work that day. He had no idea what I was talking about. I even pointed out that his yellow hi-vis clothing was torn and near shredded in places. His jeans were much the same way and his work boots were all scuffed around the fronts. But he had the blankest of expressions on his face as I presented all of this to him.

I remember Jen showing me the state of some of my clothes. But the dots weren't joining for me. They still don't.

I couldn't get my head round it in all honesty.

All of this behaviour was so unlike him anyway but it was now happening in front of other people rather than just me. I think that was the factor that scared me the most, because everyone else can judge without knowing the facts behind the madness they are seeing. I wasn't there to explain the reasons behind his behaviour, so it scared me that he was possibly being looked at like a head case.

Jen then said we should go back to the doctor.

He needed to be looked at.

We went and saw the consultant in charge of Mark's case. He told me that what was happening was probably a result of the delayed concussion from the accident. But he had to admit to me that he had never heard of a case like Mark's before.

Jen and the doctor seemed to be talking about me as though I was a science experiment. And all it has done is make me feel like a child. After all, here I am sitting in a small part of the room feeling stupid as I fill in these pages of this pathetic little 'journal', trying to remember things that I cannot remember… Sorry, Doc. Cheap shot.

Mark couldn't get his head around the fact that he had trouble there. I don't think that he really wanted to try. But what he also didn't realise at the time was that it was pushing me away from him. I never told him that. But that was the truth of it. I was very scared to be around my husband at times. His behaviour was becoming too erratic and he was acting out things that he couldn't subsequently recall.

Jen cites this period as the time where the chains came loose and we started to drift apart.

I didn't feel safe, if you know what I mean?

I felt like I was on eggshells because I didn't know how to be with my husband any more, in case he just started lashing out about something. It's hard to describe but you feel a complete stranger to the person you're sharing your life with. But then I got a surprise...

There was then a week where I just left the house.

Mark left me a note on the kitchen table one morning.

He said that he didn't like the way that his actions were upsetting me and that he felt that I needed distance from him. I was shocked because he had never said anything to me about his feelings.

I thought that it was the best thing to do.

I didn't want him to do that. He didn't need to leave the house. I just wanted answers to all the questions that I had. I wanted us to start talking about everything rather than be at each other's throats.

I went to stay with my mate, Jamie.

He rang Jen and told him I was there. I didn't speak to her because I thought it would lead to another fight and the purpose of me leaving was to avoid all that shit. So I gave her some space.

Space away from Mark was where I found what I wanted to know.

DOCTOR'S NOTE:
"We seem to have reached the point where parts of the puzzle from Jennifer's side are coming together. I think this is something that Mark was unaware of. Not being able to convey his emotions and open up about everything could have been the main cause of his own feelings of distance from his wife. We already know that he is madly in love with Jennifer but from his notes I think he feels as though he has been bullied a

45

little by actions that he simply cannot remember. And I forgive the cheap shot that you aimed at me, Mark. All this will help us towards the end resolution and I am fully aware that you are still finding it difficult to open up. For the next session, let's carry this forward and find the points of discovery. What happened after Mark left the house for that week? Was it a help or a hindrance?"

SESSION THREE

A week away from Jen was horrible.

I know that I insisted on it but I was miserable without her. I had a lot of sleepless nights.

I couldn't get used to the house without Mark there.

I felt that I had put a wedge between us because I was not accepting of what had happened to him. But I also felt ignorant of his feelings and that I didn't attempt to help him talk things through that were bugging him. Plus, I missed him like mad.

I rang the house and left her a voice message.

He rang when I was out visiting mum and dad.

He told me that he still loved me with his whole heart, that I was his world. He said that if he came back home then he would try his best to prove how important that I was to him. He must've said that he loved me over fifty times in one message. I was so happy to know that I wasn't destroying my marriage because looking back on it and everything that went on at that particular point, I wasn't very sympathetic.

Jen then sent me a text message.

I told Mark to get home. Now!

I went back home and the minute I got through the door it was like I was seeing Jen for the first time. I was all over her. It was probably the best sex we'd ever had.

My husband is my ultimate lover, hands down.

I tried my best to do all that I promised to Jen over the phone otherwise it would have been just words with no actions. I took time off work so we had time together.

Mark didn't need to try so hard.

As long as I was still with him and he wanted to still be with me, then I was happy. But it has to be said that he tried his best to pull out the stops. He took time away from the job site and handed a lot of stuff over to Jamie so that we could have some quality time together. It was really nice. The best thing was having him back in the house. I had missed him and it was an extreme that was not necessary for him to go to at that particular time.

We were then in bed one night and Jen was having trouble sleeping.

I just couldn't sleep for some reason.

I had that feeling buzzing around my head that there was something that I was missing, because although Mark was back at home, I was certain that we weren't completely out of the woods just yet.

She does worry a lot sometimes.

I did try to convince her at the time that she was over-thinking too much, but she was having none of it. She didn't understand why she was in such a state and yet she was there, trying to understand it. It was annoying because she was there prodding me to be awake so she could talk to me about it and all I wanted to do was go to sleep.

I went downstairs to watch a bit of telly.

I then saw that in the VHS player there was a tape inside so I decided to play that. It was The Avengers and it had obviously rewound itself so I was watching it from the start. I then found out what I had been subjected to from the moment that the episode title of the first episode came on the screen, The Nutshell. The minute that I saw that, the whole thing clicked for me and the fog cleared immediately.

She came back to bed a little bit happier that night, so I'm still wondering what the hell actually happened to make her sleep.

Now I knew what I was facing I was a lot happier.

I watched two black and white shows on the tape and then went back to bed. I called the doctor the next morning and told him what I thought was going on with Mark. I thought that he was acting out the episodes that he had seen on the tape. But I couldn't figure out why he was forgetting about it all when he had gone through making a spectacle of himself. That was the only aspect of the whole thing that confused me. It still confuses me now a little bit...

DOCTOR'S NOTE:
"Upon reading this section and checking the session notes, the doctor referred to in this passage had placed a note on the system and into the case file saying that he had set up scans for Mark to attend."

They wanted to look at my head to see if there was a chemical imbalance or something going on. Basically they wanted to look at my brain and, to do that, they had to place me into an uncomfortable machine where I had to hear a whirring of noises whilst they played a radio very low in my ears to try and drown out the noise. Naturally, I took the news that this had to happen to me quite well.

Mark being Mark, he didn't want to know.

There was nothing wrong with me.
I just got hit by a wrecking ball whilst having a crap, okay!

I then watched the rest of the tape in case he went through the process again.

Mark thought I was mad but I wanted to be prepared just in case another incident occurred, because at this point anything was possible and we had already had more than a few surprises.

49

Jen seemed to think that I was acting out an episode of a TV show all the time. I thought it was complete rubbish. I would know if was doing something so stupid, and I wasn't doing that. I was completely in control. It was all crap! I was being made to feel as though I was losing the plot.

I did try to explain to Mark that I was doing it all for his own good, but he was having none of it. We then had a massive argument about how he thought he wasn't trusted and that I was looking at him as though he was a lunatic. I tried my best to convince him that it was all being done in the name of making him feel better, but he was not listening to any sort of reason.

I didn't feel comfortable in my own skin.

When your wife tells you that she is watching a TV show because she needs to get to grips with what you as a person might next act out from that show in front of her, it scares you. You start to get paranoid over what you may be capable of and you also start to wonder 'why the hell can I not remember any of this?'

I had to do it.

She didn't have to do it.

DOCTOR'S NOTE:

"I am sensing a lot of passion from this session, but it's coming from opposite sides. Jennifer wants to fix a problem and Mark is distancing himself from it due to feelings of inadequacy and mental insecurity. This is a natural reaction, Mark. But as we have said, progression through ideas that you feel are a threat to you will allow both understanding and acceptance of the behaviour you were exhibiting at the time. For the next session, place the focus on Jennifer's idea. Was she right to watch the tape so thoroughly? Were Mark's fears fully justified?"

SESSION FOUR

I went back to work.

Everyone was joking about what happened between me and Jamie. I didn't know what the hell they were talking about but I went along with it. I did feel as though I was the outsider for a couple of days because everyone was in on the whole thing apart from me. It got scary for a while. It was like being drunk and having no memory of how stupid you had been. In all honesty, I would've preferred to have been drunk because that would have been more normal, something that could be explained away. But looking in from the outside, it was like I was laughing at the joke without hearing it.

Mark became a little distant at home.

He was really feeling pressure, bless him. He didn't know what to do or say to me which hurt a little. I didn't want to make him feel uncomfortable by telling him what had happened during these little episodes that he seemed to be having. But I couldn't keep from him what was going on because he would have been hurt by the fact that I was keeping things from him. I was feeling that we were separating at that point. We weren't as close as we used to be and there was practically no communication between us.

Jen and I were barely talking.

I would go out to work and then I would come home, cook my own dinner. I didn't want to put Jen out because she had been at work too. I would then go to bed and not want to really talk about anything or do anything. It's hard to believe, considering that I go to bed each night with the hottest woman on the planet, but at that time I could not engage. It was as though I was a viewer looking in on my own life. I was constantly wondering what was around the corner because everyone seemed to have their eyes glued to me. It was like I had been placed into a bell jar for everyone to point and stare at.

51

I would try hard to get Mark to talk but I got nowhere.

Even seeing me wearing next to nothing for bed wouldn't make him crack, which was unusual. But looking back on what happened and what has led us to you, Doctor, I'm not really surprised. Anyway, I continued with what I felt was the right thing to do.

Jen continued watching the tape, adding insult to my injury.

I watched the episodes thoroughly because I thought that if this ever did happen again, then I would need to know each episode on that tape to near perfection.

She treated it like a homework assignment from school.

I spent most of the night in front of the telly, which was normally Mark's job.

I felt as though I was a project for her on which I would be graded. In all honesty, I'd listen to the things she and others told me that I had done, but I'd have no memory of them. It's hard to explain, but it's like someone telling you that you snore and you telling them that it's absolute rubbish.

This was important.

There was a link between Mark's actions and what he was watching. I had the proof but I kept wondering if it would be put into practice. So I kind of ushered things along a little bit because I needed to be certain that I was onto something positive.

Jen asked for us to take a couple of weeks off work.

My plan was to try and force whatever episode was left lingering around out of him.

I booked the time off and it all seemed fine.

Much to Mark's surprise, he sort of discovered what I was up to.

I came home one day and found that Jen went out to buy some clothes.

And when I say clothes, Doc, I mean that she seemed to have gone to either a costume shop or proper outfitters.

I looked at those episodes and thought that it would be a good idea to use everything that was in them, so if Mark had another block in his memory then what I provided as a resource would help him to remember. I went out to a theatrical shop and had some pictures made of the stuff that I was after. I came back home with one of those all-in-one leisure outfits that Emma Peel (I think that's her name!) wears in the colour episode on the tape. In all honestly, I saw myself in the mirror and thought that I looked like Sue Sylvester from Glee. But out of all of it, Mark's was the easiest to get hold because let's face it, how many men in this world don't wear suits for business or everyday wear?

She had brought me this gorgeous suit.

It really was a good suit. It had a velvet style collar and I was really happy about that because they were coming back into fashion. Plus, she had got the suit pretty much tailored to my measurements, so it fitted me like a glove.

He was always playing the central lead character in his little escapades, so I went out and bought the smartest suit that I could find from a charity shop. It was actually a custom tailored suit so I was surprised that someone else had Mark's measurements. I think that the gods were smiling on me that day!

It looked great. I still have it.

I then bit the bullet.

Jen said that we had to go out in these clothes that she had bought!

Mark was more than happy to go out in the suit.

Jen felt very uncomfortable.

I could feel everyone looking at me. It was embarrassing. I looked like I was stuck in a time warp even though what I was wearing could easily be mistaken for something trendy. But I had a good reason for it and I stuck with it.

DOCTOR'S NOTE:
"We have a breakthrough moment here. It is quite clear from these notes that Jennifer took some positive action towards helping her understanding of Mark's problem, which is healthy. It provides a clear picture of how strong you both wanted your marriage to remain. For the next session, focus on the outcome of the dress-up. Was it right for Jennifer to push for a result and was the reaction what she hoped for? Is Mark any closer to remembering his actions?"

SESSION FIVE

During the time I had off, Jen kept wearing that one outfit.

She then insisted that I do the same thing. It was a bit annoying because it could be a hot day and I was sat there in a bloody shirt and tie, sweating my bollocks off. I have seen people that do this for a living in every form of business, but even they get to take their jackets off or remove their tie. I was instructed not to do this so I was there losing about half my body weight with sweat pooling in my shoes.

I didn't know when Mark would next burst into a TV play.

I had to cover all the bases, so I asked him to keep the same clothes on every day. I washed them each night and ironed the shirt every evening, so everything looked good. I know that he was bugged by it very much. So was I, if I'm honest. It's not very normal to ask your husband to behave abnormally to their own nature, but at the time I didn't think that I had any other option.

We would be going out to do a bit of shopping and everyone would stare and point at us. Kids were the worst because they would be coming home from school and they would be shouting jibes at Jen looking weird. I personally thought that she looked hot because the outfit she was wearing was figure hugging in areas.

Mark did think I looked good.

So, if anything, a positive in all of this was that I was keeping my husband interested in me whilst looking like an utter idiot, as I endeavoured to sort out his medical problem.

I then apparently caused the biggest fight since our marriage began.

It finally happened while we were on the way to visit my mum and dad.

Mark was driving along the road and he kept going into places where we didn't need to go. He then called me Penny – and it clicked that we were now entering the world of The Avengers again.

I have no memory of what I apparently did.

DOCTOR'S NOTE:
The Avengers – DEAD MAN'S TREASURE (1967)
"Steed and Mrs Peel become involved in a dangerous game, participating in a car rally the purpose of which is to track down a great treasure. The trouble is, some of their fellow competitors are prepared to kill to win."

It was interesting, looking back on it now.

At the time, though, I was embarrassed beyond belief. He was driving around the town as though he was going around on a treasure hunt, just like they did in the episode on the tape. We were going around streets with a lightning accuracy and he kept going on about a man called Danvers and how he had left a secret message that Mark had to find.

I couldn't really enjoy myself because I knew what was happening now and it was making me think that it was some form of brain damage that was going to get worse. It was a serious accident that happened to Mark after all, so it could've have given him a split personality.

We then kept bumping into friends, which didn't help things for me. Here we were trying to catch up with friends and Mark was standing there looking at them as though they were characters from a Sixties television show. What do you do? We didn't tell everyone about the accident – and these were long standing friends of ours – so the only thing I could do was to keep chatting away and hope that they didn't take too much notice of Mark and the vacant look he was wearing.

Jen has told me this story.

We must've driven along the whole town in one afternoon. We pulled up at some odd places; I think one of them was a pub where he was staring at the

56

sign, looking for a clue. I even shouted at him, "What are you doing?" and he looked at me with that same vacant expression. It was like talking to an absolute stranger.

We don't know everyone in the town.

Mark did take us to places I had never been before, like the other side of the town.

But he then took us down a country road and was treating the traffic as though it was the two enemy agents following him. He even said that the windscreen had been shot at.

What can you say? The more outlandish he seemed to get, I had to follow him, so the only thing I could do was sit there and agree.

I had to humour him a little bit at one point and said, "Don't worry, babe. Next time we'll buy the bullet proof screens." I remember after saying that to him I wanted to die. I felt like such an idiot.

I remember coming home. That's all.

We got back after nearly emptying the car of petrol.

Mark pulled up and saw our neighbour's car in front of us. He got out and began looking it over, which he had never done before. I wanted to scream at him, "It's a Ford Sierra, Mark! Leave it alone!"

It's a great car. Old school model.

He kept looking it over as though he was searching for woodworm.

Then our neighbour Matt came out of the house and saw Mark looking it over. He immediately said to Mark that it wasn't for sale, but then Mark went at him and asked him where the treasure was.

I don't believe that I attacked Matt. He's a nice guy and we've always been good mates.

I'm standing there and watching Mark try and get this answer out of Matt, who is looking absolutely petrified. I then remembered what happened in the episode and said to Mark that the treasure was in the car. "Look in the boot," I screamed at him. I just wanted him to snap out of it.

Jen then says that I apparently looked in the boot of Matt's car for something.

The trick worked. I got Matt to open the boot of the car and go along with what he was seeing. There was nothing in there, thank God. But I then saw Mark come back to reality when he saw inside the boot.

By that point, everybody is looking at us in the street. People have come out of their homes and are wondering what the hell is going on. I just made my apologies to Matt and got Mark into the house.

Jen dragged me by the collar and screamed at me when we got into the house.

I was livid.

I didn't mind the odd drive around the town and to the places where he thought he was getting a clue for his so-called treasure hunt. But attacking our neighbour and embarrassing me in front of the whole street was a step too far for me. I know that I was probably in the wrong, but it was the principle of the thing.

She slapped me across the face and stormed out.

I hit Mark because I was angry at the clothing element not working.

I thought that by wearing the outfit to fit the episode or show he was acting out, it would help him remember his actions. But it didn't and it just looked like I had dressed him up so he could go ahead play acting.

I still to this day have no idea what I did.

Looking back now, it must've have been difficult for him.

She made me apologise to Matt.

I had to explain to Matt what was going on and how the accident had given him a few problems. Thankfully, he understood.

I didn't know what to think.

My wife was telling me that I attacked my neighbour; my neighbour is telling me that I wanted to find something that wasn't there in the boot of his car. I just didn't know what to think. I thought I was going crazy.

I didn't help Mark in that period of time – I know that now.

Who is more responsible for the distance between us? I would have to say it's half and half.

Jen put the distance there.

She kept me at arm's length after this incident with Matt. I thought it was because she fancied him and we had another fight when I brought the subject up.

Matt is a married man.

I know his wife Nicola very well and we started spending a lot of time together after the attack. But, with Mark not being in on everything and seeing me get pally with the neighbours, he assumed that I was having an affair. It was complete crap!

I did feel threatened.

My wife is keeping away from me and she keeps telling me about everything that's happened during her day and it's involved her spending time with another man. What was I supposed to think?

Mark was then starting to get a little worse.

The dress up idea backfired on me in a very big way after that.

I don't know what happened, but I've been told that I went through a radical change.

He started looking at all of these old cars in magazines and online.
I knew that this stemmed from The Avengers and all I could do was go along with it. I knew that he had the treasure hunt episode buzzing around his head, and, although it had caused me a lot of embarrassment, I thought it was a good episode. But the fact of everything is that Mark was trying to live a fantasy rather than deal with reality.

I was clearing some stuff out the other day and I found over seventy copies of magazines about vintage cars. I don't remember buying them.

He was deadly serious about buying a vintage car. He was all for it.

I don't believe for one minute that I was going to buy an old car.
I like the one that I have, plus I never went in for museum pieces. They're fun to look at and clean, but from what Jen told me I was thinking of driving one around the whole town.

Can you imagine it?
Doing your food shopping in a vintage 1926 Bentley convertible?

It's a nice idea and I think Jen wasn't exaggerating when she told me that I was serious about doing it. But in all honesty, Doc, I cannot remember anything about the whole event. As I've already written, I can't even remember buying the magazines.

He subscribed to them through an online ad.

They just arrived at the door. There were bundles of magazines, full of pictures and details about all sorts of beautiful vintage cars. Honestly, Doc, they were gorgeous. They had chic lines, the sun was glinting off every picture, and the way in which they were all presented definitely appealed to me. I love cars and seeing so many stunning machines fed my soul. But I have no idea how I came to own one. Jen will tell you different, but it's true, Doc, I had no idea that I had picked up the phone and paid out for one of these cars.

The first sign I got that he had done something was when I checked the bank statement that we have for the house bills. It was considerably down from its total and I had no idea why. A week then passed and there was loud knock on the door. I wondered what the hell was going on and was met on the porch by a man in overalls saying that my new purchase was being delivered.

I was upstairs when I heard my name screamed in a very angry way. Jen was not happy with me at all.

On our driveway was a green Bentley that cost him over £20,000.

I saw this wonderful beast on the drive.

I looked at Jen and I swear that I heard her screaming voice drift away to be replaced by the sound of this fantastic new car begging me to take it for a drive.

I was livid.

All of that money was kept by for urgent bills and he went and spent it on a car that, I later found out, was from a museum showroom. He also used some of his company funds to help fund this personal purchase, something he swore he would never do when he had started the firm. This big impulse buy meant that money was short when it came to paying for job site materials or staff salaries.

I did try to reason with Jen, saying that I had no idea how I managed to buy this magnificent car, but she was having none of it. We became the talk of the street because it seemed like we were going to give them all a show – and it was to be my death at bargain price.

I was becoming a curtain twitcher because I was suspicious of anybody wanting to intentionally scratch the car and void the warranty on it. I know that Mark was going through some crap, but of all the stupid things for him to have done...

I then decided that we should take the car out for a spin.

The moment that he said he wanted to take the car out for a drive I knew where it would lead. This was still in the dressing up phase of things so there was only a certain amount of time before something came along to make the package look complete. Against my better judgement, I agreed to go out with him for a spin. I should've said no, but I just went along with it.

Doc, this car was amazing.

There were a few teething troubles to begin with. I had never driven a museum piece, but the basics were still the same. The trick was in learning how to double-declutch, but I'd read up about on Google, so I was quite confident. Pleasingly, I managed to slowly get the car off the drive and into town.

He drove the Bentley okay, but that was because he was doing it gently.

I told him not to go mad at it and we slowly drove around the streets so that he could get the feel of it. I know he wanted to keep it, but there was no way I was going to be paying off a twenty grand debt for a vintage car.

Things then apparently came to a head.

We were in the garden.

It was sunny day and I thought we could take advantage just by having some chill time together in the front garden. It was common to do this in our street because everyone had barbecues and we sometimes made a group effort of it with our neighbours. Anyway, we were just sat there and then I saw that look come across Mark's face.

Within minutes he had ushered me into the Bentley. I was scared stiff because I knew that this was not going to be the sort of pleasant drive we'd had before. He started the car and I screamed at him to let me out. But the minute he called me Penny, I knew where his head was at. Thankfully, we were still dressing up in all of the Avengers gear, but once I tell you this story, Doctor, you will see why it wasn't the best idea to wear it on this particular day.

Apparently, I did some damage with the Bentley.

He could barely steer the car properly the first time around, even when we were just pootling along at 20mph, but this time things were even worse.

He found the hand brake and stomped on the accelerator and we nearly went into the wall. He then eventually found reverse and forgot where the brake pedal was as he was moving so we ended up in the garden of our neighbour opposite. We crashed through his fence and demolished his prize-winning roses.

I am a superb driver.

I cannot believe for one minute that I caused the destruction that Jen told me about. And I cannot take seriously what she said happened when I took it for a spin, either.

He drove the Bentley into town.

I was trying to keep my head down because I was dying of embarrassment in the passenger seat. The Bentley is a convertible vehicle, Doctor. We could be seen quite clearly as my husband tore up the road, trying to work out the clutch and gear lever. Then, I heard the sound of sirens blaring out because my husband was driving at 60mph in a built-up area.

Did my husband stop? No. He kepr going, declaring that he is being chased by enemy agents.

I have no memory whatever of the incident.

The petrol tank wasn't that full, thank God.

Mercifully, the car ground to a halt just before we hit a tree and we were taken to the local Police Station for questioning because the police officer who found us thought that Mark was drunk in charge of the vehicle. I did try to explain the situation, but was told that it would have to be sorted out when we got to the station.

I don't remember being at the police station.

It was a nightmare.

Every time that the police asked Mark for his name I had to correct him because he kept calling himself John Steed. He actually thought that he was a character from a Sixties TV show. What could I say? We were hardly the best picture of sanity at that point, being dressed up like two people headed for a costume party. Things got worse the more that Mark was questioned because I had to correct everything that he said. The interviewer then left the room. I took the opportunity to try to shake some sense into Mark, who was acting as though he was being interrogated as a spy.

I kept looking at the ceiling wondering what I had done to deserve this. I was very worried about my husband's mental health because it was the first time that I had ever heard him say that he was John Steed rather than Mark Gardiner. I explained to the interviewing officer about Mark's consultant at Nullington hospital, outside town, Dr Constantine. I was praying for them to get in touch with the doctor to straighten this whole mess out.

Doc, I am not deluded.

I am Mark Gardiner. I have never ever claimed to be somebody else. That is, I don't remember ever claiming to be anyone else.

We were there for hours.

I told them all about Mark's accident on the job site so they had information they could check with Dr Constantine and verify that it was Mark. It took them hours to get through to him. They were thinking of getting their own medical man involved but I wanted them to speak to the person who knew our case. I didn't want Mark looked at by another doctor, only to be locked in a cell for the night. It was bad enough that we had been there for hours already.

I remember coming home.

I found myself driving the Bentley along the road and I asked Jen where I was.

He snapped back to himself as we drove home.

I couldn't speak to him because I was that angry. I wanted him to snap out of it while we were at the station, but could he do that?

64

She didn't speak to me but I soon recognised where we were. It was a thrill to drive that car. I was having a ball, but judging from Jen's manner, I guessed was in for the screaming match of a lifetime.

I persuaded the police to let us take the Bentley home.

Mark jumped at the chance to drive it because he was still being Steed at this point. I wanted to throttle him because he had turned what should have been a nice, relaxed day into a complete nightmare. He parked the car and I didn't speak to him for the rest of the night. I chucked the clothes that I had brought for the dress-up idea into the corner of the bedroom and didn't want to see them again.

I hadn't expected things to spiral out of control in the way that they had. I thought it was going to be a simple exercise of playing dress-up to cope with these little dramatic outbursts with the Avengers. But it backfired in a major way. To top it off, we now had a vintage Bentley on the driveway.

Jen told me that I could stop wearing the suits every day which I was more than happy about. I didn't like wearing them in hot weather. I did speak to her about the Bentley, though, because I wanted to keep it.

That vintage car was the symbol of how bad things were with Mark at that point. The last thing that I wanted to do was for us to hang on to it. I made him return it at the first opportunity. But that wasn't the only thing that had a backlash effect on me.

Jen became self-conscious about going out in the street.

People had started to look and point at me as I went out, due to the incident with Matt.

I was even stopped in the street by someone who had watched Mark go for him and who had seen us going shopping whilst wearing all the gear from The Avengers. And she just looked at me and said, "Who was that man I saw you with?" I pretended that Mark was a friend because I didn't want to admit to the whole thing. At that point I had a hard enough time admitting it to myself, let alone anyone else, especially neighbours that we hardly knew. She believed that it was all a stunt between friends. She replied, "Very good looking man. If I was younger, I'd be in there!" So in the process of my utter humiliation, my husband pulled an older woman!

Things weren't the same from that point.

From my point of view, my husband was changing completely.
The difficulty that stemmed from that was that Mark had no idea what was going on and I was the one getting at him for changing so radically. The harsh factor there is that I really did not give Mark any form of chance. I was too wound up about it all.

The fights were becoming a little bit fiercer between me and Jen.

She would be pointing out this weird shit that I would be doing and I wouldn't have a clue as to what the hell she was talking about, which would make her more angry. And then I would get angry because she was getting at me for a reason that I had no idea about. In reality, I felt very much attacked.

There was a part of me that thought we could work things out.
I know that it doesn't seem like that from what I'm writing, Doctor, but I truly wanted me and Mark to work through this.

Jen being so picky all the time did make me think that our marriage was over.

There are only so many times that you can take the blame for things; some you know are down to you and others that make you feel a target. I reached that point and I didn't see a way out of it. There would be days where we would barely talk and just go to each other's place of work. We would get home and be in separate rooms. It was horrible.

Mark was giving me the silent treatment.

I didn't know what to say. If I did say anything to her I would get my head bitten off! So, I chose not to say anything at all.

DOCTOR'S NOTE:

"We have reached one of the crucial points of this case. The incidents that are being described by Jennifer are the obvious manifestation of the doctor's warnings regarding Mark's accident. But what I can pick up from this is that Jennifer is not exercising any patience for her husband's actions which had caused the initial friction between the two of you. The foundation of your marriage still appears to be solid in what I'm reading, which is very positive, but it's clear that patience is what was needed at this time and it had been exhausted in both of you, for whatever reason. For the next session, did this situation get worse? Did the distance between you widen?"

SESSION SIX

I finally railed against the silent treatment.
I couldn't keep being quiet with Mark any more.

Jen started talking to me one night over dinner.

She had made one of my favourite dishes and offered it as a kind of peace offering. But we didn't really cover what we needed to address. It seemed to me as though she was still attempting to avoid the issues that were bugging her. It was obvious to me that she wanted to just break the ice and test the water for a conversation, but I was still treading on eggshells. How can you convey that to your own wife? What do you say to her? "I'm sorry, darling. I can't talk to you because whatever I say to you is never what you want to hear. I don't know what to do and feel self-conscious. So I'm going to shut up…"

I didn't know how to approach it.

It's really something when your husband is acting out these little plays for everyone to look and laugh at and he forgets them the moment that it's all over in his head. How are you supposed to deal with something like that? Looking back, I think that it's a good thing that he did forget what happened. I don't think that he could live with himself!

I did try to take into consideration what Jen told me.
I couldn't believe it, but I did listen.

Things did continue to get worse rather than better.

There were more stories from the job site at this point, I remember.

Mark had been given the go-ahead to build an extension to our local cinema.

The work was much needed money because my company was busy handing out redundancies left, right and centre. We needed the money and Mark went out and got it. He was always someone that got up and did what was necessary when he needed to.

The cinema job was a good one.

He was working regular hours, which foxed me a little at first.

I spent most of the day at home and I was flicking through the TV channels. I decided to look on the Sky planner to see how much room there was available on it. I was a little shocked to find that The Avengers had found its way onto the planner via the True Entertainment channel. I had no idea this was going on. Only one of the five recorded episodes had been viewed and I was wondering when Mark had time to do this. I did what I had done before – I quickly ran through the entire episode at 30 times speed. It seemed to be an odd episode and it was just a quick flick through anyway. I stopped it at a point where Steed was apparently dead under a pile of rubble only for him to appear out of nowhere and have a fight. I was still amazed that Mark had recorded this and not told me.

But I put it out of my mind and waited for Mark to come home as usual. He was a little angry and told me that he had been sent home again.

I asked why and Mark told me that his foreman was taking the heavier load. I didn't question it at the time. But then the bubble burst on the reason for it.

I would get to work in the morning and Jamie would meet me.

He would always give me a sheet of paper that marked out when I was to leave the site. I'm the boss and I'm being told when I can go home? I wanted to punch him.

Mark told me this and I called Jamie.

Jen wasn't happy when I told her that I was being undermined by my own staff.

I met with Jamie and then he told me the reason why everyone wanted Mark out of the way at a specific time. Apparently, Mark had been going through more episodes away from home and it was bugging everyone on the job site.

I heard about what I supposedly did on the job site. I asked Jamie about it, after the event, obviously.

From what I was told, I believed it.

Jamie told me that there was a near incident involving a forklift.

Mark was using the machines on the site like they were part of the treasure hunt episode that he had seen and it freaked everybody out.

There was also an incident while we all had lunch.

Jamie told me that Mark was in there once and was just talking to Geoff (a chippie) and he was treating it like an interrogation. From what was described, it sounded like the episode on The Nutshell.

I don't remember this.

Jamie said to me that they were worried about Mark.
They all got on with him and they knew that this was not normal behaviour. But when he got home, he was his usual self. In all honesty, I was glad to palm the weird behaviour off on everyone else rather than deal with it myself. It sounds selfish, but I really needed a break from dealing with it.

I was being sent home quite frequently.
I took it up with all the guys and they told me everything. I got scared at that point because now it wasn't just my wife telling me that these events were happening, and that hit me like a lightning bolt. Plus, Jen then showed me that *The Avengers* was on our Sky planner. She had frozen the episode at the point where a fight had occurred on a building site of some

kind. That's when it really hit home for me. So, I decided to do something about it.

Mark then pushed for medical checks.

I was worried for my health.

I thought that I was going crazy, and I needed it to be sorted as soon as possible.

The doctors put him through for the scans required.

It was the same as before. There was no head damage or major trauma. It was a waiting game that we had to play out. But I didn't want to do things in that way.

Jen wanted answers.

She didn't want to hear that we had to wait until all of this passed.

You were right, Doctor, I had no patience.

Looking back, I wish that I had, because I was taking things out on Mark, and on the doctors. I was yelling at everybody because we had been down the same path so many times, and I thought we deserved to hear something other than the words, "It'll pass in time..."

So, rather than wait and feel bored with the whole process of the NHS, I decided to try and do something else to aid the situation.

Jen suggested alternative therapies.

She began to get in all these different flavoured teas for me to drink. They tasted like hot water with no flavour at all.

I did fill the cupboard with everything possible.

All I wanted was for Mark to live out all of the stuff he was acting out in his dreams, because that way I didn't get a call from the job site saying that his behaviour was freaking them out again. I just knew that I had to do something. I was tired of waiting to be told by a medical professional that my husband was better when I knew better than they did. It seemed as though they did not want

71

to do anything at all. So, I got in all of the special teas and home brews that I could find. I went shopping for all the alternative gear. People must've thought that I was trying to exorcise a ghost or do some other weird thing. But, at the end of the day, this was for my husband's own good.

It was quite an exercise!
She still hasn't got rid of them all.

Some of them are nice!

DOCTOR'S NOTE:
"I'm sensing urgency here. Jennifer wants to be rid of this thing once and for all, rather than be patient (which I am pleased to see that you now recognise; this is a healthy step taken), but Mark seems to be a victim of his own actions. He has no idea what is going on and yet is still being told that he is behaving oddly. His lack of descriptive narrative is showing signs of his insecurity."

Bullshit!
I just can't remember everything that people are telling me I was responsible for. It has nothing to do with my feelings or anything else that you quacks keep on pointing to. My behaviour has put me into this situation and I want out of this bloody thing fast! Writing stupid notes to be looked at like I was still in school! What good will those do in fixing my marriage? If you ask me, this whole process is a crock of shit!

DOCTOR'S NOTE:
"Here is the anger that you have been hiding, Mark. Scribbling out all of my previous notes just to make this little addition was the manifestation of all the pent up rage you've hidden and held onto. It's okay to feel anger. You have been through a traumatic event and are being told things that your conscious mind cannot

fathom at all. Please, I'm here to help both you and Jennifer through this. The events that you are telling me about will help everyone in understanding the path to revelation, fixing the problems in your marriage. It might seem a futile exercise to you at the moment, but I'm here to help."

I hate when he's difficult.

DOCTOR'S NOTE:
"For the next session, did the actions from the job site return to the home? Mark being difficult is making me sense that we have finally broken the shield he has put up, as you both seem to be revealing the shattered state of your home life, which was once strong and unbreakable. What caused the foundations to be rocked?"

SESSION SEVEN

Mark went off on one again.

Jen says that I was the one who made her leave the house permanently. I don't believe this for a second, because she was the one that was always getting bent out of shape over things. Half the time she was barely talking to me.

I just couldn't take it anymore.
I was walking on eggshells when around my husband and I hated it.

It happened one evening, or so Jen claims.

We had some friends over that we hadn't seen in ages.
It was a good night. Mark cooked dinner and we both had a really nice time. We never really got much of a chance to socialise with friends, not since the accident, so it was really good to be a couple and entertain as though it was the norm for us.
I suggested that we also have a few drinks, because it really had been a long time since me and Mark had been able to let our hair down. Then our friends, Gary and Rachel suggested party games to liven things up.
I thought I'd dig out Twister, because that's always a laugh. Mark always cheats when he has the turn of the board and makes sure that he puts me in the most awkward position possible. I asked him once why he does that and he told me it was so he could purposefully watch me. Even playing Twister, he checks me out!
But we were in the middle of Scrabble when things went mad again. I was close to winning the whole game and Mark was not himself at all. I could see in his face that we were due another explosion into the world of The Avengers.
But it never happened. I was quite surprised.

We went to bed and I didn't think anything of it. I was an idiot for thinking that, but we live and learn by our mistakes.

Then it happened. At 3.00am, Mark woke up. He went downstairs and I didn't see him until about 5.00am. He had gone out in the car and came back with a jigsaw puzzle. He had left it at the old flat and had gone all that way in the early hours to pick it up.

He then started to put this puzzle together and kept going on about it revealing a house. The picture was the Manchester United logo, so I knew that things were not completely okay with him. He was busy with it so I left him and went round to my mum's.

About an hour later, he arrived at my mum's and started treating her like she's the enemy he's been searching for. He kept referring to Miss King being missing so I knew that we were in for another portion of The Avengers. I told my mum to go ahead with whatever he says and told her what he was going through. The key to it all was to humour him, but I hadn't banked on everything else in the bargain.

My sister's kids were around at the time and they thought it was a great laugh as he went through the back garden as though he was playing the secret agent game from the episode that I remembered from the tape.

DOCTOR'S NOTE:
The Avengers – GAME (1969)

"Steed's past comes back to haunt him when members of his former regiment are murdered in a series of games. But when Tara King is kidnapped, Steed has to go play the same deadly game in order to save her."

It was embarrassing.

My mum watched from the kitchen window and was laughing to herself. She thought it was a real giggle that Mark was treating my niece as though she was stuck in a giant hourglass and that he needed to rescue her. He kept telling her that the sand was filling up the glass and that she would nearly be buried in it. He then pulled out a fake gun and shot her free. I didn't know where to look.

They then started to fight invisible people! They were at it for about half an hour, just punching and kicking the air like a load of lunatics at a rave party.

I'd had enough at this point.

I then apparently hit my head again.

He tried to perform an invisible hit and lost his balance, knocking his head on the ground as he landed. I checked that he was okay, in spite of being at the end of my tether with him.

I woke up on the ground and was being escorted into the kitchen by Jen's dad who had just got back from visiting a friend.

My mum and dad were looking after him but I had to get out of there.
I had taken enough of this crap from Mark and that episode was the last straw for me. It's not easy to see your husband go through something like this and then not be able to talk through the whole thing with him because he has yet another bout of memory loss. I had nobody that would understand what I was going through because, as far as I knew, nobody else's husband had suffered the effect of a wrecking ball hitting him as he took a dump in a portable toilet.

Her mum and dad couldn't fathom what had got into Jen, but she stormed out.

They were very nice to me and told me what I had been doing in the back garden with the grandkids. I couldn't believe it, but I knew that they wouldn't lie to me.

I did think to myself that Jen had left me there out of sheer embarrassment, even if the kids did enjoy it.

I went home after the aching in my head had gone away and found that Jen was in the process of packing her bags.

I couldn't live with him anymore.
I did try to reason with myself as I drove home, but I was already set to leave. I simply could not be there anymore. I couldn't stand it any longer, wondering when he was going to burst out and perform another episode.

I did try and plead with her not to go.

76

Mark was very pushy about me not leaving, but I already booked the taxi to my sister Rebecca's.

I was on my knees, I remember.

He did beg me to stay, literally. But I wanted out of there.

She was gone and I didn't know what to do.

DOCTOR'S NOTE:
"From Jennifer's perspective, she had taken a lot on board due to Mark's accident. I can clearly understand why she felt the need to leave the family home. But through these initial sessions I feel as though Mark has not been able to fully express his feelings after the accident. His side of the story is important and the repetition of reading that he knew nothing about the effect his behaviour was having reveals that he did not have a proper outlet to vent his frustrations. I have an initial outline of his feelings, but in order to progress further, we would have to go deeper. For the next session, both of you individualise your thoughts from that period. Let each other know how you felt at the time, in the form of a letter to that person and be expressive, because in the next session you will read them to each other…"

SESSION EIGHT — THE LETTERS

To Mark,

I've never written a letter to you before, except when we were in school together, so please forgive me if I get this all wrong. I need to be honest and clear. We have a great relationship and I couldn't have picked a better man to be my husband. You're one of the sexiest men in the world and the best part of it is that you're mine. You always take the time to tell me how important I am to you and what our marriage means in the long run. I'm always grateful for this because it reassures me that you think of me and where our relationship is at.

Looking back at what happened to us and what led us here to these sessions, I think that I may have been a little judgmental. I clearly did not consider feelings at the time that I am considering now. I do not feel guilty about any decision I made back then because being with you at that time was difficult. Every time I would try and speak to you about things, you would turn it into a personal war with me. I didn't want to keep fighting you and the more we fought, the more wild you became, so I left. I know that I hurt your macho pride by having you beg on your knees for me to stay, but I didn't want to be fed the line of 'I will change…' Every man says that and most of them don't bother because it's too hard for them to even try. It's not that I didn't believe that you would try, but I just needed to get out of the house and away from your 'episodes'. They were becoming far too frequent and it was getting very difficult to explain your behaviour to everyone, and to friends in particular. The family understood the problem, but when it was happening in front of everyone, and we were both being made a spectacle because of it, is where I wanted to draw the line. So I did and would do so again, if necessary.

Your behaviour was so erratic, and I was unable to predict what you would do next. You became someone that I didn't understand or could not fathom at all. I kept wondering what would pop up next and would be living day-to-day with a chart in my head as to how serious the new day could be compared to those previous. I was worried about what to say in case a word triggered you off. It's hard to describe everything, but all I will say is this; it was like living with your Uncle Peter.

You once told me that your Uncle Peter was a man who seemed to carry a thousand personalities in his head and it would excite you seeing him when you were younger. But as you grew older, it became very disturbing for you, and how you longed to have a normal conversation with him. You have become your Uncle Peter. You had this accident at the job site and it had turned you into someone that had stored episodes of a TV show inside your mind and you were doing nothing but play them out at the most inopportune or embarrassing times. Also, just like Uncle Peter, you would call people by their character names and assume that they had the traits of the fictional people that you had invented. You were acting out episodes from a television show that is fifty years old and that is now not generally well known. The people you inflicted your fantasies on have probably never even heard of The Avengers TV show. You hear the word Avengers, and you instantly think of the Marvel incarnation of it, which then springs the idea that you would act like Captain America in the middle of the road, which would be equally embarrassing. The only saving grace about the TV show is that you're not wearing spandex or carrying a weapon that could get you arrested. After all, nobody can arrest someone carrying an umbrella, can they?

I know that you will hate my likening your condition to that of your Uncle, but it was the only way I could explain clearly how you were freaking me out. Acting out episodes from a Sixties television show to anybody, and then not knowing what you had done afterwards, was something that I couldn't understand. I still don't, if I'm honest. It still bugs me that you have no idea of it today. You were the one that was acting stupid, after all. You work on a building site; surely someone would have videoed it for a YouTube exclusive?

I was frightened. I thought that you were losing your mind and developing an alternative personality that would rear its ugly head when I least expected it. That was the part that scared me most. We could've been having an intimate moment together and then all of a sudden you would burst into a spontaneous action and become a different person. I didn't want that to happen.

I left you because I couldn't take the insecurity of everything any more. I didn't want to keep biting my tongue around you and treating you with kid gloves whenever the problem flared up once again. It was affecting your work, and it was affecting us. People at work were ringing me to tell me that you were having these weird delusions and I had to tell them not to call a doctor because you would snap out of it when the episode you were playing out was over in your head. They just had to be patient. I realise that I should've listened to my own advice, but where in what I just revealed is that normal? I should've insisted that a doctor be called out to see you, but you would have been put in the nuthouse. That is why counselling is the only option that I could see for us. Talking about things can open up so much and I needed to open up to you and have you listen to me rather than turn things into an argument all of the time. It was not good for us to keep doing that. For one thing, you are far too stubborn and sometimes never accept the fact that you are in the wrong. I had to keep guessing whether you really could not remember anything about your behaviour, even though I knew that you were not lying.

I realise that coming to these counselling sessions was not what you wanted, but we have to do something to save our marriage. I have not stopped loving you, nor will I ever. But I want us to return to how we were. I hope you do too.

All my love, Jennifer xxx

To Jennifer,

These sessions that you have dragged me to so that a quack (sorry, Doc!) can analyse what is wrong with me have been interesting. It's made me feel smaller than I could ever have imagined. And it's apparently all my fault. It seems like there is an unfair mantra that is playing throughout the whole of this and it's always coming back to me. I cannot understand why this is and would like you to explain it to me.

I have gone through the ringer; I have been hit by a wrecking ball whilst I was trying to peacefully sort out a crossword puzzle on the toilet and found myself auditioning for the builder's version of Superman. Do you take this into consideration? Do you believe that you could be more open-minded when it comes to the oddness that has obviously stemmed from my behaviour? No, you don't. Instead, I have to deal with the brickbats that you want to keep hitting me with.

I don't deny that I have some blame to take for the way in which I made parts of our marriage crumble, but I can't take the full brunt of it all. You put in a couple of punches yourself with all the screaming matches and the ways that you used to tell me how embarrassed I had made you look in front of everyone. How the hell was I supposed to know what I was doing? I still don't know about it all now. Even when I would ask you to tell me, you would look at me like something that had just dropped out of a dog's arse. All I wanted to know was what had happened.

I'm not calling you a liar, babe. That's the last thing I would do. But what I am saying is that I don't think that you had or have any sympathy for what happened to me on the job site all that time ago. I did not go to have a crap with the intention that I was going to be flung across a car park and land in a bush with the safety net of a portaloo to cushion my interesting fall. It didn't help that the actual loo whacked me on the head so hard that it gave me a scar across my eye. I'm also thanking God that the lid to the thing was shut, as it did somersaults around my noggin. I performed very tight cartwheels in a box with my trousers round my ankles. In other parts of the world I would've won a medal.

I honestly think that you don't understand or want to understand what I went through. At the doctor's appointments that happened after, you didn't ask me if I felt okay or if anything was wrong with me. Instead, you have screamed at me and told me stories that I have been acting weird and dressing weird with it. May I point out that the dressing up fiasco was your idea? I didn't want to dress in a suit during summer but you insisted! What the hell did I do wrong there? All I did was to follow your instructions and I get the blame for it. We never talked about anything after the incident occurred, and that was all down to you. You wanted things to return to normal and have me just carry on as though nothing had happened. Well, it didn't work that way. I went through absolute hell and you're still making me pay the price for it. It's because of the hell that I am now writing you this letter like a schoolchild trying to contact an invisible pen friend. We shouldn't have got to this stage because if you talked about it with me it may have been sorted.

I don't deny that my behaviour caused you to leave the house. But where was your understanding there? I was begging you to not leave and to see if we could both work through this. But no, you decided to be selfish and leave me. That hurts, Jen. My behaviour is the root of this and, yes, I do think you're right that we need to do something to help out our marriage. Our bed is too big without you, so come back and we will sort this out.

Love, Mark xx

DOCTOR'S NOTE:

"Having written and read these letters out to each other, you both seemed to connect again as a married couple. There was some eye contact made during this first consultation in the same room together but I still feel that there is a fractious air between the two of you. There are still some issues that need resolving and approaching before we can enter the next stage of proceedings. For the next session, return to your private notes and concentrate on the fallout of Jennifer leaving the family home. Did Mark's attitudes change along with the distancing of the odd behaviour that drove her away? Does he want to change things?"

SESSION NINE

Hang on a minute, Doc!

Yes I want things to change. I want my wife back in my home and in my bed. It's been over two months and I'm missing her. You make it sound as though she doesn't want to come back unless I offer a divorce as an option.

I'm not treating this as a game, you know. This is my marriage and we're writing in these pointless books to try and sort it out. And what is this next stage? Are we going to strip naked and not touch each other because we're both having a fantastic time of doing that now. Honestly, you doctors can be so condescending.

Mark and I have been living in separate homes for a little while.

I do want to go home. I miss him like mad. But I still face the problem of going back into the arena to face him acting out another episode of The Avengers. It's too weird for me and I understand that it's not his fault. But back then I just wanted to be out of the house. I have been advised that time is a healer, but I keep wondering when the right time will be. I don't want to rush back into things and then have it all fall around my ears. That's not fair to me or Mark. We need to allow the time and the distance to breathe some fresh air into things, whether we want to or not.

I have spoken to and seen Jen since she left.

She asked if we could go slowly on things because she did not want to move back immediately. I begged again. I felt like a dog wanting a treat but, yes, I begged and pleaded with her to come home and I did it because I wanted to be back with my wife. I had obviously done something wrong and I wanted to make the best effort I could to repair the damage. But all it did was to scare her off.

Mark has been very sweet about things.

83

I can't stay away much longer. It's not fair to him and he has tried his best to make me feel comfortable around him again. He has called, texted me and he's been very sweet each time. I admit that I was put out when he begged me the second time to come back home because I hated seeing him like that. He looked so pathetic and was not the strong man that I married. I reduced him to this and I couldn't deal with that on top of everything else. But he has been sweet and he has shown me some understanding.

I wrote her a massive essay of a letter.

He gave me this letter which seemed about 80 pages long.

He wrote about our first date and how he missed seeing me first thing in the morning. He was very sweet and, the more I read, the more it was convincing me to go home. The routine of home life was definitely something that we had both been missing and we were only now starting to acknowledge our feelings. By the third page of the letter he had me, but I did read the whole thing.

I also wrote about missing sex with her.
What? I want my wife, is that so wrong?

He got a bit naughty after the fifth page!

I just want my wife back.
I'm willing to do anything, Doc. I even have plans in my head about what I would do.

DOCTOR'S NOTE:

"Excellent progress has been made here in this particular session. But we have already established that you both want to re-connect as a couple and that will happen in due course, rather than overnight. It is healthy to see that you both want the same thing for your marriage and this will help us. The item we still have to address is the last two months of your separation. For the next session, let's cover the events of Jennifer leaving. Mark has demonstrated that he would go to certain lengths to win his wife back; did he do this immediately? Or did Jennifer make the first move?"

SESSION TEN

I went to stay at my sister Rebecca's.

I could have gone to Mum and Dad's, or even my other sister, Natalie. I wouldn't go to my brother Michael's. He loves Mark to pieces and would instantly try to play matchmaker if he knew we had split. He's very sweet but I just wanted to get my head together. I felt as though I had turned traitor on my marriage but I still believed that a little distance was the key to hopefully solving everything.

I had a lot of sleepless nights.

I didn't sleep for about two weeks and I was buying beer like there was no tomorrow. The corner shop had a section in the fridge that was especially for me. Over eighty cans of beer for just me and I got through at least fifty in one week. I was very isolated and shut out the rest of the world. The phone would constantly ring and the messages would be from Jamie and the guys at the job site. I just wasn't interested in doing anything. I closed the curtains and drank for England, crying because I had lost Jen.

The first few nights without Mark were hard.

Everyone in my family had looked at us and thought that we were solid as a rock. Rebecca has three kids from a failed marriage, Natalie is flitting from bloke to bloke with an alarming regularity, and Michael has been engaged to the same woman for over fifteen years. I was the one that finally took the plunge and made the ultimate stand to say that I have a marriage that works and I'm going to keep it that way. They were not expecting me to turn up and say, "Guess what guys, it ain't working for me either." I didn't say that but it would have been what they were thinking. Rebecca was a great comfort. All of my family love Mark and they wanted us to patch things up as much as I did, so having that was a real help and a comfort to me. My misjudgement about their reaction was cleared up there and then. I discovered it was because I was the

86

only one outside of mum and dad that was married. They wanted it to stay that way. I have a charming family!

I tried to ring around her family and they were all protective.

Nobody was giving her whereabouts away to me and I was trying my hardest to wonder where she could be. I was amazed that nobody knew what was going on. I thought that they would have been told the minute that it happened. It always happens that way, doesn't it? You have something happen and it whistles along the family grapevine singeing the ears of everybody that wants to listen.

Rebecca did tell me that Mark had left messages every day for me.

I left messages everywhere that I called. I was really annoyed because I couldn't talk to her. I couldn't even hear her voice when I wanted to; at least that is what I would shout to myself.

So I just opened up another beer and turned the television volume to maximum level. I was creating a bubble for myself to protect my own emotions. I would watch telly until I fell asleep in front of it. I would wake up next morning feeling like crap and just open up another can and choose another channel. The bubble was becoming my sanctuary, such was the depressed state that I found myself in. I wanted the world to leave me alone but it wasn't that easy. The hurt would not go away.

I left it about two weeks before I messaged him.

I didn't want to appear to be too eager and I was also nervous because I knew that he would be directly at the other end of the line. It sounds weird but I was getting butterflies in my tummy just thinking about hearing his voice.

Jen sent me a text.

We met up for about ten minutes in the park and barely said anything to each other that was worthwhile. We sat at opposite ends of a bench and heard nothing but the wind in our ears.

I kept a distance from him. I didn't even give him a cuddle, which tore me apart inside. Looking back on it, I can't believe I was that cold. But that was how bad things were. I had no idea where to start with him and I think that he had the same problem.

I got all nicely done up for meeting her.

I had a shower and didn't drink for two days. I put on a shirt and wore my best aftershave. And what for? Just a quick hello and to see her walk off, leaving me in the park looking like an utter twat!

I think I hurt him on that first meeting. I didn't intend to do that. I did want to talk. But the minute that I saw him in a shirt I was remembering him jumping around my parents back garden like an over-hyped schoolboy. It was a powerful image and I had not been able to distance myself fully from the episodes that he had been acting out.

Yeah, I went home feeling really good about myself that day.

I burned the shirt the minute that I got in. I didn't want the memory of my wife looking at me in pure terror and then running away like a frightened rabbit, thank you. So, I went straight back to the beer. I had been turned down by the hottest woman in the world and I wasn't feeling very good about it.

Rebecca then got my mum and dad in on the whole thing.

I didn't want them to get involved because it was my mess and I didn't want everyone trying to offer about eight million opinions on what to do. But I sat down with my parents. They reasoned that Mark had been through a very difficult ordeal and that I needed to think hard about what had happened.

The television was becoming my best friend at this particular point. I wasn't the sort of sad act that knew the ins and outs of every character on *Eastenders* (although that was a favourite of mine with *Coronation Street* as a fantastic second) but I knew that I was becoming something that I wasn't. I was a shadow of my former self. I hated feeling that way. It was crap. You look around at once at what was once a beautiful home and realise that it's now covered with empty beer cans and the half eaten remains of Chinese takeaways. It was a tough sight to take in. Really tough.

Mum looked at me. She told me about how she and my dad went through some rocky patches when they first got married and that every marriage has its highs and lows. Although I was happy to have my mum giving me advice, at the time I didn't want to listen to it. I was still reeling from the fact that I was treating my husband as if he was a stranger to me.

I didn't go out to work for another two weeks.

Jen leaving and then the whole meeting up thing going sour had hit me hard. I was drinking far too much and I didn't want to see anyone. I didn't open the curtains for over a week because I didn't want to let the daylight in. I just kept staring at Jen's picture on the wall and willing her to come back to me.

Of course I wanted to go home.

I missed Mark like mad. But I wanted things to return to how they were before he'd had his accident. I wanted to return to normality. I was too busy being selfish, I suppose.

I was out in the pub one night.

Jamie came in and saw me sat in the corner. He bought me a pint and we discussed everything. It was not an immediate release, but Jamie did eventually tell me that my behaviour was a worry and that it put a lot of things into perspective from everyone else's viewpoint, because they had been worried about me for a while.

I then asked him about the stories that Jen had relayed to me. He confirmed the facts in each one. I knew that nobody was lying to me but I just wanted to get my head around the situation. I was being a kid after all – you know what I mean, Doc? I was acting out fantasies like a child without a care in the world, only to completely forget that I had behaved in that manner.

Jamie came back to the house that night and we fell asleep in front of one of the adult channels. I woke up next morning and we kept chatting about my problems. I found this surprising as Jamie had never struck me as the sort of fellow who you could talk to on an emotional level. For him to be going over all this with me was a real eye opener. I could finally get everything off my chest to someone who was willing to see my side of things and not be prejudiced against me.

And it wasn't a guy thing, if you know what I mean, Doc? We didn't sit there and curse womankind as a horrible creation, or attest that men were better off on their own. I was just confiding in a friend about the fact that my gorgeous and beautiful wife refused to come home to me, and how the incidents and our separation had ruined my life... It hurts to even write that down.

I had been at Rebecca's for over a month.

She would listen to me whine and moan about how I missed Mark. She'd then argue that I was doing nothing to sort things out and get back together with him. She was right. I was being a coward.

But, in a way, I was doing it to prove that I was worth something in Mark's eyes, if that makes sense? Looking back, he did try. I ran away. So as I think on it now, I do ask myself what the hell was I wanting from him?

Dad had always said to me when I was growing up that Muhammad sometimes has to go to the mountain. And it wasn't until this point in time that I realised what the heck he meant by it. But I chose to do nothing. I wanted to be chased by my husband. I wanted him to run after me and prove to me that I was everything to him. Looking back, I was being more than a little unfair, because he was already demonstrating that.

I was starting to not want to be at home.

I was living at the pub, or so it seemed!

The days were bleak. I only existed in two places, eating only when the mood suited me, and just drinking the world away. Jamie tried twisting my arm into coming back to work because there was a lot of stuff on. They needed an extra hand and although he had done a brilliant job filling in for me while I took sick leave. But I couldn't face going back into work with everyone knowing that Jen had not returned and that we hadn't patched things up.

As a result, my routine was always the same. I'd sleep in until gone 10.00am. I wouldn't eat anything until lunchtime when I'd go to the pub and buy myself one of their huge food platters, enough to see me through the whole day. Then I would buy my first pint of twelve at the bar. Most days I'd leave the pub at about 9.00pm, go to the corner shop and buy myself around a dozen cans of beer. Then it was back home, where I'd crack open a beer (or two, sometimes three), put on a movie or flick through the channels, and fall asleep in the chair, drowning in my unhappiness.

I never slept in the bed. I would make up the chair in the front room, because the bed was for me and Jen, together. Sleeping there, alone, would have made me even more depressed. I would have stopped eating altogether and just carried on drinking until the corner shop barred me as a customer. I was getting to be quite a regular in there, so they had my order ready the moment I walked through the door. That sort of thing is fine at times, but in this instance, it wasn't for me. They knew I was washed up.

I wasn't living at all. I was existing, but for all the wrong reasons. I was very lonely, melancholic and alcohol dependent.

I got to bond with Rebecca a lot at this point.

We were always close but we never had the chance to really spend quality sister time together, which sounds a little strange coming from someone with only a few siblings. But one day and she just turned to me and asked me what I wanted to do. Did I want to divorce Mark?

The answer was obvious; no. I wanted Mark to be my one and only for life, no matter what. But now I look back on it, I realise I didn't give him much of a chance. I had been sympathetic but only to a point. And if I want to analyse it (sorry, Doctor, I know that's your job), I should've been a little more supportive towards him. But I think everyone comes to a point where they know that they can't cope any more, where the stress of a situation becomes overpowering. I still think I was right to leave Mark. I needed space to breathe and consider where I was in my marriage. What I think I was wrong about was the length of time I was away from Mark and breaking off the communication between us. I cut myself off from him and placed the two of us into a divide. We didn't know what we were both thinking or wanting and that was hard on both of us.

I did keep checking my phone in case he messaged me but he didn't know that was what I wanted from him, so it never happened. I then got a call from Jamie about the business. The owner of a place that they were building an extension onto wanted to meet the man in charge (my absent husband) to talk over further possible projects. From a financial point of view, it would be great for me and Mark, and Jamie was calling to make sure that he got his own slice of the profit cake as whilst Mark was away he was calling the shots. I think he was secretly revelling in Mark being away, something which disgusted me, in all honesty. Here we were, in the middle of a marriage crisis, and Jamie wanted to line his pockets rather than be the friend to Mark that he always claimed he was.

He then told me that Mark had become something of a bar fly. It shocked me a bit to hear that he was drinking so much, but I did put him in a spot where he could see no other option. After Jamie rang, I did think of visiting him at the pub he was going to and making a play for him, where he could pick me up and take me back to the house. But the only guarantee in doing that was that we would fuck each other's brains out – we wouldn't sort out the problem. Even though I was missing him physically, I wanted a solution more than sex. I wanted things to be sorted a certain way and the problem that I engineered for myself was that I had put Mark into the role of the chaser.

I woke up one morning and looked at myself in the mirror.

I hadn't shaved. I was red eyed from the 18 cans that I had consumed the night before. My head felt as though a truck had rolled over it. I spent a whole day sat in the chair, staring at a picture of Jen. I had reached a new low in my life and I hated it. I was becoming a full-on drunk.

My days away from Mark were spent wasting time.

All I did was go to work, spend some time with a bottle of wine while chatting to Rebecca about how I hated the day, and go to sleep. I think I was doing exactly what Mark was doing, but not in the same way. I was depressed about the state of things and was looking for the perfect release. I found it at the bottom of a bottle. It was easier than it was to pick up the phone and try to sort things out.

I did think about contacting Jen.

I knew where she was and I could easily have called her, but I was scared. I didn't know what she wanted me to say to her. I didn't even know what the hell I wanted to say to her. I knew I wanted her to come home but I had already begged her to until I was blue in the face. She still wasn't interested. So I left it alone.

Rebecca went to the house to fetch a few more of my things.

Jen's sister came for some of her clothes and things.

We ended up chatting about things and I found myself unburdening a little. I don't know why I did, but Rebecca seemed to genuinely want to know how I was doing.

My sister came back to me with a clear message.

She told me to get out of her home and go back to my husband.

I refused.

I still wanted to be chased and wanted proof that Mark was committed to making things work between us. Looking back, I glossed over the fact that he had been in a serious accident that had affected him. I think I just wanted some time to be in the spotlight for a change, rather than the focus being on Mark all the time.

DOCTOR'S NOTE:

"Excellent progress has been made here. Mark, you have really opened up. You have admitted that you could see there was a problem in your behaviour after Jennifer left and have been open about your reaction to it. And Jennifer has done the same by admitting that she was feeling pushed aside by the focus being on Mark all the time. Selfishness is necessary. Marriage is about togetherness but it's also about the individuals

93

and their need to be free to express what they want to their partner. I am sensing that outside forces were attempting to fix the problem between you. For the next session, focus on how you both reached a resolution. Who made the first move? Who opened the lines of communication?"

SESSION ELEVEN

I returned to the pub.

But I slowly cut back on the beer. After speaking to Bex about Jen, I saw how bad I'd let things get. I didn't like what I was doing to myself. I was worth more than that. So, once I'd begun to lessen the drinking, I went back to work. I arranged for some big business that would keep me and my men working for a few years, thanks to a few new names that had arrived in the area. I had to console Jamie a little bit because I think he had enjoyed me being away a bit too much!

I tried returning home.

I chose to take a day off work and visit the house. I was nervous about doing it but I really wanted to see Mark and how things were, considering I had been away from him for nearly two months.

I entered the house and Mark wasn't there. I was shocked at the state the place had been left in. There were takeaway cartons filling up the bin in the kitchen, the living room was covered in empty beer cans, and the smell of the place left a lot to be desired. I think Mark had been just wallowing and that was my fault, I hold my hands up to that. He needed understanding at a time when I didn't give him any.

I went up to the bedroom and found that was the cleanest room in the house. The bed hadn't been slept in.

Although I was nervous about seeing him, I waited for an hour in case Mark came back. I tidied up a bit, considering that I was in my own home and my husband was treating it like a pigsty. I then left him a note asking him to ring me.

I came home from work and found the house had been cleaned.

It was weird.

I then saw a note from Jen on the fridge asking me to ring her at Bex's. I waited for a couple of days before I picked up the phone.

95

I finally heard Mark's voice again.
I broke down. I'd missed hearing it so much.

Hearing Jen was like listening to angels.

I think she was crying on the other end of the line. I hoped she wasn't because I don't like it when she cries.

We chatted for hours. It was so nice.

The phone call with her was unlike any other conversation we've ever had.

I think the only thing that we didn't mention or discuss was the accident that happened, and that told me that we were still okay. You get to that point where you just know that you can move on from something and that conversation pointed out that there was still something there to be saved.

I didn't want to be reminded of what Mark had gone through.
We had been told about it far too much and technically we were still living under the trauma of it. This was just a phone call so I could test the water, so to speak.

I didn't ask Jen directly to come back home.

I don't know why, because I really did want her to come home, but I had a strange feeling that the answer would be no. I didn't want to be pushy about it because I was still in the process of becoming me again, so to speak. With that in mind, I left the subject of her coming home alone.

I wanted to be back with my husband.
I know that I've been saying that I was testing the water and that I was nervous about going home, but the point I'm making is that I was made to feel a stranger in my own marriage. The man I married had become a different person due to the accident and his spells of madness were unpredictable. It really unnerved me because I didn't know how he'd behave from one minute to the next. The worst part of it was that it wasn't Mark's fault. So the test part of

things was to find out whether I was going back into tiptoeing on eggshells or if there was a basis for some form of normality?

I tried to be as understanding as I could with Jen.

I loved her still and made sure that she still knew that before she hung up the phone. But I knew that I had to do something to convince her to come home. She wasn't going to come back because I wanted her to or she wanted to. She had to feel safe in her own skin and her own home. I understood that right from the beginning and now that I had put the beer to one side, I could try and work with that factor.

As I write this, I realise how selfish I was. It's disgusting that I couldn't be as sympathetic and understanding with my husband as I should've been. But I think that other people might see my point of view and realise that to understand that sort of situation fully, you have to have been inside of it yourself. I think that by being self-centred it allowed me to keep my perspective and remind myself that I was just as important as Mark was. But, in hindsight, the level of the selfishness could have been toned down a bit to give Mark a fair chance. But now we had reached a talking stage, I kept it going rather than run away.

After that first call, Jen rang a few more times.

It was always nice because I would get home from work and just sit down in front of the telly and the phone would ring. She would tell me to eat a proper dinner rather than just make a sandwich and we would talk until we were both ready for bed.

My mum and dad told me that we were acting like teenagers. Odd really, considering that Mark and I never did this as teenagers! But there was some truth to what they said. Both of us were a little bit stuck on getting started and were waiting for the other person to make the first move.

It was a reconnection.

Jen had been out of the house now going on three months and I chose that time to ask her directly to come home.

Mark then asked me to come back.

I thought it was stupid for us to be separated like this.
Everything could go back to normal when she came home.
But she was having none of it.

I didn't say no.
What did happen was that I was reminded of what I had been made to go
through before I had left the house and I told Mark that I didn't feel
comfortable. And that didn't go down well.

I got angry because I felt that I couldn't win.
I was trying my hardest to make things okay between us and she was
putting up this brick wall that I couldn't break through.

He hung up on me.

I didn't get it.
I was guilty of all this shit that had gone on and my wife had left the
house because of it. I have no memory of the things that made her leave and
she won't come back and work out our problems. What the hell was I
meant to do?

I didn't ring for a couple of days.
I felt that I had done a little damage just as we were starting to reconnect.

DOCTOR'S NOTE:
"The feelings of wanting to be together and the
attempts at re-establishing connection with each other
are very much in evidence. This is very healthy and you
both seem to be allowing yourselves to be more open in
the writing of your notes, which is helpful to all parties.
For the next session, focus on the reunion that the
notes inform me occurred between you. Who initiated
the two of you becoming a unit once again?"

98

SESSION TWELVE

I had been working flat out.

I was taking a lot of work home with me so that the building accounts and other stuff didn't fall through the cracks. I wasn't eating a lot and I was going to the pub less than I did before, so I was getting quite tired. And one night I came home. I put my work on the kitchen table and I just sat in front of the telly. There was nothing on and I noticed the video was indicating that there was a tape still in there.

I took it out and saw that it was the *Avengers* tape from ages ago. I don't know why I'd held on to it but I had. I also had the episodes of the show piling up on the Sky planner thanks to the True Entertainment channel. I still cannot understand how they got there and there was still only one of them that had been viewed.

I put the video on and watched what was on there. It was difficult because there were some black and white ones on the tape. I don't handle black and white too well. I get fidgety because I think that sometimes not having colour can slow down the pace of whatever you're watching. It's like if I went to see Bruce Willis in another fantastic instalment of *Die Hard* and it was in black and white; my brain won't allow me to connect to it.

So I sat there and watched this tape. It was quite good. A little hard to follow in some places but it was a good show to watch. I like the character name of Steed. I'm sorry, but you hear that and you would immediately grant someone respect with that name. I started to get into this show which was odd because it wasn't of my generation. It was from the 1960s and anything that was made in the 1960s was made to last forever like *Star Trek* and its follow up shows, *Mission: Impossible* and its own movie series, *The Prisoner* and everything that goes on with that show and its fans (I saw a documentary on ITV once, Doc. It was all about how the fans showed their appreciation for the show and the character of Number Six. Not bad for a man who kept telling everyone he wasn't a number!)

This was my dad's sort of show and I can see why people would like it. I watched the tape a few times in that week because I was getting the feeling that I had been here before, if you know what I mean, Doc? I felt that all the scenes were personal to me and I just couldn't figure out the reason why.

I was missing Mark so much.
I was missing him emotionally and I was definitely missing him physically. I rang him once or twice after the incident where I shot down his offer to come home (you idiot, Jennifer!). I don't mind telling you, Doctor, that at times the sound of his voice caused my juices to bubble (now blushing at having revealed that to my therapist! What am I doing?).

Jen rang a few times.
It was always a pleasant conversation between the two of us and I was missing her so much that I didn't want to hang up the phone each time. I got the feeling that she wanted to sort everything out but, because I had driven her out, it was my job to bring her back. (Wow! Look at me with the knowledge!)

I wanted him.
I wanted him as my husband, I wanted him as my friend and I definitely wanted him as my lover.

When Jen rang again on another day something happened.
I felt as though I needed some answers and the only way that I was going to get them was by asking her directly what it was that I did that caused her to leave. She then told me that it was all about the *Avengers* tape that was left in the machine. I was apparently regularly engrossed in it (I don't remember this, but seeing the tape recently I can see why I would be). She then told me that it went further than she had let on – and how she played dress up with me to try and help me to remember the things that I had forgotten during my escapades (Jen's words, not mine!). The dressing up part I remember but I didn't remember the other stuff that had occurred and that I had to be informed of.

100

Jen then said that she had studied the tape herself and that I was acting out everything that appeared on the tape. And for her, it got to the point where she had done that one time too many and I was getting more and more into the world of the show.

I then started to remember why I was feeling as though I had been here before and it came back to me that I had religiously watched this tape already. That was the only thing that came back to me at that point. I was hoping for more. I was desperately hoping that I would remember some of the events that had been described to me, but nothing like that happened. All I was remembering was that I had seen this tape over a million times. How could I forget that?

I would ring Mark a lot.

Each time it was like I was falling in love with him again, it was amazing. But he then kept bringing it back to what made me leave him. And I asked him why he was questioning me so much about it. And he just said to me, "I want to fix this". It made me cry. Sorry for being so emotional, Doctor, but he was being so sweet in accepting that his behaviour drove me out of home that I felt like such a bitch for walking out.

I came home from work one night and sat in front of the racing.

I don't know what made me watch the results or even record it onto the Sky box but I did. And as I saw this, I remembered something that Jen had told me about the old cars and the magazines of cars that I used to keep.

I then went out to the garage to grab a beer. We've got another fridge in there where we store our reserves of beer and wine. The house is designed in such a way that if we ever run out of drinks, we can just pop out of the back door and enter the garage by its side door rather than go around the front. I opened the door and switched on the light and just stared for a moment at the Bentley that I had bought. I remember that I had to beg Jen to let me keep it in the garage, but I have to admit, Doc, that I did tell a little white lie about having the car recalled. What? I loved the car and I still didn't care that it had cost me twenty grand.

I decided to jump in behind the wheel – I really felt at home there. I imagined taking the car for a spin and whisking Jen off to a small country retreat where we would have mind blowing sex. We would then talk through the night before returning home and carrying on as if none of this rubbish was happening. But I have to admit that sitting behind the wheel of the Bentley made something happen for me.

I don't know anything about things like selective memory or anything like that, but a light just came on in my head. I started to remember being dressed up and going through this process of trying to dredge up some memory of the flashpoints my mind was keeping from me. It was like I had just entered the Twilight Zone. It was freaky that I had forgotten just how engrossed I was in this video tape, but I still couldn't remember anything that I had done. I remembered being dressed up like a dog's dinner in a smart suit when it was, like, thirty degree weather outside but I still don't remember acting out the things I had watched.

I made up my mind that I needed to properly talk to Mark.

I had fought it long enough and if it was going to lead to the bedroom straight away, I wasn't going to complain! I wanted to shag my husband, is that wrong?!?

I started to watch the *Avengers* tape again.

I watched all four episodes and squirmed through the black and white ones, trying to keep up. Thank God they were good stories.

I even chose to watch some of the episodes that had been recorded on the planner, even though it's a mystery to me how they got there. These ones were all in colour and it was easier for me to keep focused from start to finish.

But I then figured out what I was going to do to get Jen to come home and it was *The Avengers* that inspired me.

DOCTOR'S NOTE:
"Mark has really opened up in this session and it's nice to see that he was the catalyst for the reunion. Jennifer, do not be embarrassed by being open in your

102

comments. These notes aid the sessions that we have and they allow us to sort things quickly. With this in mind, we will return to the reunion soon. Right now, what has struck me is the honesty that has been tapped into about that particular time. For the next session, construct another letter remembering the feelings that you had towards each other and your situation from that point. Be honest and open with each other."

SESSION THIRTEEN — THE LETTERS

To Mark,

I missed you and wanted you so much. It had been three long months that I had been away from you and with every phone call you were making my heart skipped a beat and my juices were flowing like a river.

I wanted to get you into bed and mount you all night long. I wanted to feel your lips all over me like they used to be. I wanted to feel your arms around me and feel so secure. I wanted to be near you and watch you stare at me when you thought I didn't notice. I wanted to remember what it was like to be your wife again.

I was missing being with you. The routine of us both working and managing to unwind every night in each other's arms was the biggest thing that I missed.

I know that it was me that forced us to live apart, but I had to get some space to clear my head. I just didn't see it becoming as long a separation as it did. I had only intended to be away for a week or so. I know that it felt longer and believe me when I say to you that I was going through the same pain that you were too. I wanted to return but I was scared that I was entering the same situation that I had run from. I expected to come into the house and find that you had transformed it into a shrine to The Avengers. I imagined that you had chucked out all of the clothes that I love seeing you in and switching it for a wardrobe full of tuxedos and suits that wouldn't look out of place on James Bond. It's not that I have anything against John Steed or 007, but I would prefer the man I married.

But when I came back to the house to finally speak to you, it was nothing like I had imagined. If anything, the place looked like a tramp was living in it. It was a complete and utter tip. You had turned one room in the house into a pit that even pigs wouldn't be seen dead in. I was expecting the whole house to be the same. And then I saw that you had gone nowhere near our bedroom.

Strangely enough, it proved to me that you had remained the man that I married. It made me want you so much more.

My main focus at that point as to try and fix the problem that I had caused. I should have been more sympathetic to you and understanding of what you were going through because of your accident. I was not sympathetic. I was judgmental and selfish in the process. I wanted to come home to you and wanted us to be the couple we should have been, but I also wanted to feel valued and wanted you to pursue me. I wanted you to prove to me that you wanted me back as much as you would tell me over the phone.

All I can do is apologise if you feel that my actions made you feel inadequate and please believe me when I say that I wanted you back.

All my love, Jennifer xxx

To Jennifer,

I wanted to know why you refused to come home. I was trying everything I could think of to convince you to comeback. It's our home, after all, and we should both be living in it. I just wanted you home so I could hold the hottest woman on the planet in my arms again.

I missed you so much. I would stare at our wedding picture on the wall and just want you to leap out from it and wrestle me to the ground. I wanted to taste you all over and feel your soft skin on my lips. I was missing being able to stare at you whenever I wanted. I was missing looking at your body as it tried to burst out of your clothes like a water balloon at full stretch.

I was lost without you. I had no idea what I'd done to make you leave our home and I really wanted you to come back to me. I would've done anything for you and you know that's true. You are everything to me, Jen. You always have been, right from the moment that we met. It was killing me that you wouldn't speak to me about it.

I didn't want to force you to come home. I would never do that. But I did want you to think about me and my feelings on the matter. It did seem to me that you had just left without giving me any indication as to what it would take for me to even speak to you, let alone get you to come back home. I was still trying to work out together exactly why you walked out of the house in the first place. It was sod's law that I would start to piece it all together when you had well and truly left the house. But I did try and I begged more than once for you to come back. I didn't want to push any more than necessary and I apologise if I did so. I just wanted you to come home.

I was nervous about ringing you. But you put all my worries away when we started talking again. But you didn't have to avoid the subject of coming home so much. Whenever I would bring it up you would quickly change the direction of the conversation. I wanted you back but you didn't want to know about it. That hurt me.

I did succeed in winning you round again but at the time I wanted you to just listen to me. There was no need for you to be so defensive or offhand about it. It's our home and I wanted us to be one again.

Love, Mark xx

DOCTOR'S NOTE:
"There are some very honest feelings revealed in these letters. Both of you wanted to reunite but there was still the question of Jennifer needing to feel wanted and valued. Mark, you stated in your letter that you succeeded on winning back your wife. For the next session, let's focus on the reunion, so that we can consider what brought you back together, and work on keeping things on a positive track. How did you succeed in winning Jennifer around?"

SESSION FOURTEEN

I was watching this tape of *The Avengers* again.

I just thought to myself that, if it was this show and my attitude towards it that caused Jen to leave, then it was a good idea to try and get her back by using the same show.

I also began taking an interest in what the True Entertainment channel had to offer. It had a major downside in the way of adverts mid-way through a fantastic episode but, to tell the truth, Doc, I was surprised that I was watching the show at all.

I remember, one week I phoned Mark and his words were, "You'll be home soon. I know it," so that revealed to me that a strategy was forming in his head.

I had to plan the whole thing carefully.

I went out to the shops in town and looked at the DVD shelves and scoured everywhere to do a bit of research to help with my plan because the four episodes that I had soaked up in my head after the accident had made Jen leave. I needed some more inspiration so I decided to look at some more episodes to see if they held any ideas for me.

Contacting Mark became a little weird.

Every time I would call him, he would sound like a schoolboy on a school trip and I knew exactly what that meant; he was up to something. It was a good job that I knew he wasn't having an affair as otherwise I would've killed him!

I couldn't find what I wanted.

I was getting so angry because I knew that there had to be some out there without having to go online for it and spending God knows how much money that I didn't have.

He then asked me over one evening to help out on a business issue.

107

I got told that there was an irregularity with a job we had previously done.

He wanted me to go over the books with him.

Jen had always been good with figures, so I asked her if she would mind helping me out with this issue because it seemed as though we would have to involve solicitors if we found that the irregularity came from us.

I agreed to do it.
I went over and we looked over the books together.

She was on one side of the kitchen table and I was at the other.
We looked like a couple of teenagers studying for an exam – it was quite funny.

I hadn't been that close to him for a while and it was really nice.

This was still at a time when she was uncomfortable being at home, so to speak.
I had previously made clear my feelings about Jen coming home, so I bided my time and didn't try to reinforce them at our meeting. After we finished, finding that we were not to blame for the business problem, she then surprised me.

Mark had been so patient with me.
I felt that he needed to know that I would come back to him, so I got ready to leave and gave him the snog of a lifetime.

She planted this kiss on me and we were stood there for about ten minutes. I didn't want it to stop.

He held me so tightly. It was amazing. But he was holding back, I could tell.

Jen says that she knew I was holding back because I didn't do what I normally do when I kiss her. In one way, she's right and, in another, she isn't. She's right because she took me by surprise and I was trying to be nice and not scream at her, "Get your kit off and let's shag all night!" And where Jen is wrong is that if I really wanted to hold back, we wouldn't have been kissing.

I went back to Rebecca's that night and started to pack.

That kiss told Mark what he needed to know and it opened my eyes to a few things too. The first one was obvious because I wanted to make love to my husband and I had missed him physically. The second was the realisation that I had been very selfish in regards to my wants and needs because I didn't give Mark the chance to fight his corner, so to speak.

I went to bed that night wanting Jen so much.

We had not been that close in so long and it was like a breath of fresh air.

But typical of the way things sometimes are, Mark became busy with work.

I knew where it would go if someone didn't hold the reins.

Jen would have easily returned to me at that point if I'd asked her to, I knew that. But I wanted to prove to her that I genuinely wanted her there for us. I didn't want her to think that I was going to use her for a quick fuck and a fumble. She's my wife because I want her all the time, not because she's an object that I can use.

We carried on telephoning each other through most nights in the week.

It was nice because we were slowly reconnecting and that was what I was after at this particular point. Apart from Mark's body, as well!

I got back to the plan instantly.

I couldn't find what I was looking for in the shops without going through special orders and it was always a chore because even then it was never guaranteed that you would get the order you wanted. And it was while I was visiting my mum and dad that my dad pointed out that I was the only person in the world (he thought) who still had a VHS player. It was only a comment, but it was one that inspired me.

I went to a discount entertainment store which catered to all forms of video – VHS, DVD, Blu-ray and even Laserdisc. And I looked around on their shelves for any sign of *The Avengers*. And there it was; a box set of VHS called the Movie Commemoration Set.

There were then a few nights that Mark seemed side tracked.

I was attempting to grab any ideas I could from these tapes.

It wasn't easy to get through the black and white episodes – and there were six of them! And none of them hit the spot for me because they didn't have anything that I could impress Jen with, and that was what I wanted. The episodes I was watching (and I did watch them, Doc. I may have squirmed a bit, but I did watch them!) were good to watch but I wanted the ideas to spring out at me.

There were four tapes in the set and I watched one tape each night. The first tape had nothing I could use, unless I tried searching for an unbreakable mug for Jen's morning coffee.

DOCTOR'S NOTE:
The Avengers – IMMORTAL CLAY (1963)
"Steed investigates a murder at a pottery as his latest assignment deals with the verification of an unbreakable ceramic material. With the help of Cathy Gale, he discovers that the world of pottery is more cut-throat than expected…"

The second tape in the set was okay but I couldn't grab anything from it in spite of how good the shows were. I could easily be Jen's butler for a day and then take her to lunch on a train (a real train and not a fake one like in the last episode on the tape). But where we go on a train is beyond me. We didn't know anybody that was a train ride away!

DOCTOR'S NOTE:

The Avengers – WHAT THE BUTLER SAW (1965)
"Steed becomes a butler as he and Mrs Peel attempt to find a leak of important secrets where the link appears to be the servants of the house..."

The Avengers – THE GRAVEDIGGERS (1965)
"Steed and Mrs Peel investigate blackouts at an early warning radar station and have to link the factors between a recently deceased scientist and a hospital for ailing railwaymen..."

The third tape was in colour.

But none of those ones appealed either because they were too outlandish. One of them was about people's fears and I didn't want to scare Jen into coming home. So tape three was a no go area.

DOCTOR'S NOTE:

The Avengers – THE FEAR MERCHANTS (1967)
"There is a lot to be scared of when Steed and Mrs Peel investigate the plight of the ceramics industry and find that the competition is being frightened out of their minds."

Finally, four tapes in, I found what I wanted.

It gave me the perfect way to start fully connecting with Jen again. It was another colour tape and it was an episode about how you could use a mirror to eavesdrop on somebody.

DOCTOR'S NOTE:

The Avengers – ALL DONE WITH MIRRORS (1968)
"Tara is sent in to discover why there are leaks occurring from the Carmadoc research establishment and finds that the secret lies in the power of a mirror."

Mark rang me and asked me what I was doing that weekend.
I told him that I was having a few days off work and he got very excited by that for some reason. He then gave me specific instructions to meet him.

I got a few friends from the site to help me out.

I got a large table from my mum and dad's that they wanted to scrap but I persuaded them to give it to me for a few hours. I borrowed a red table cloth from my mum and bought candles. I then arranged everything with the restaurant. They were to deliver the meal to the house, complete with instructions about how to prepare it. It was going great.

Mark's instructions were odd.
They led to a place off road and the area I was driving into was a little village that I had never been to before. I'd heard of the place because Mark had done a lot of building work there, but otherwise it was new to me.

Jen then arrived and I could see that my instructions were obeyed completely. I had even gone as far as to tell her what particular dress to wear.

Mark wanted me to dress as though we were going out.
I wore my black backless dress and didn't wear any underwear in case we had another moment together. I'd refused him once, so I wasn't going to refuse him again.

Her face was a picture when she saw what was going on.

I wish I had brought a camera that day because she looked bloody gorgeous.

Mark went to town on it all.
He was standing in the middle of this gorgeous buttercup field. It was amazing. There was nothing but a sea of yellow. I didn't think a place like this existed. And in the middle was my husband, standing next to a fully laid out dinner table, topped off with two burning candles, on a bright, sunny day! He

was also dressed up for the occasion which made me think that he had definitely planned all this to the letter.

I collected her from the gate and led her to the table.

It was so romantic.
He had put two roses at my place at the table. He had ordered this massive meal from one of the restaurants in the area. I was so shocked by it all. It really was amazing.

We had the meal and really did enjoy each other's company.

After the meal had been eaten I just then spent the rest of the afternoon looking at Jen. She looked amazing and was still as beautiful as she was when I met her.

He then told me that he had stolen this idea from The Avengers.
I couldn't help but laugh. It was such a romantic gesture and the fact that he took lead from the show that caused me to leave him was something I found very strange but at the same time very sweet. It was an amazing day and I fell in love with Mark all over again.

DOCTOR'S NOTE:

"This has been a very enlightening session. Mark's idea for the reunion was indeed an inspired choice and it was evident from the notes that I read that the two of you were ready to reconcile. It was nice to read that the two of you had met in the middle and showed that there was no animosity. You could be in each other's company and you could forget all of the problems that had occurred. This is very healthy. For the next session, we will focus on the aftermath of the reunion. Was there trouble in paradise?"

113

SESSION FIFTEEN

After we had dinner in the field, Jen came back home with me.
No exaggeration, Doc, it was the best sex I've ever had.

I leapt on him.
It was amazing. I finally managed to get my husband back.

Jen moved back into the house.
This was about a week after the dinner in the field and I helped Bex
move back all the stuff she had taken out from our home. It was wonderful
to have Jen back.

Mark and I entered a certain rhythm when I came back.
It wasn't like it was before. We were communicating a whole lot more – as
we had done in the phone conversations – and we were making time for each
other.

I was more than happy to give work over to Jamie to handle so I could
spend some time with Jen. I was just so happy that she had come back to
me.

Mark started to involve me in things a lot more.
If he had a decision that he needed to make about something then he would
allow me to know what it was. We would take the whole thing apart and carry
on from there. We became more of a team than we had been before and that
was nice because we had really drifted apart after the accident. Now he was
involving me in the business side of things, while letting us just be ourselves at
home, and this really showed me that he had grown in our time apart. It was
really nice to see and be a part of.

I went back to the doctor's and got myself checked over.

114

I was given the all clear, so I was hopeful that I would not be relapsing into any further weird episodes. But getting the okay was brilliant because I could do things that I was restricted from doing before. So, it wasn't long before I went back to work and earned the big bucks.

It was rosy for a good period of time.

I was a little worried by Mark going back to work, but we couldn't survive on canned food. It was only when he allowed work to take over his life again that things became something of an issue.

My being the sole king of the hill with my business sometimes didn't sit well with Jen.

There would be times when I would have to keep her out of things because I was being territorial. It's my business and I wanted it to flourish, so I just had Jen deal with the books and keep an eye on material expenditures and so forth.

But, in doing that, it left a bitter taste in her mouth. I think I'd made her consider the whole thing as a joint venture when it wasn't. I did try my best to clarify everything, but it would always end up in an argument.

He would start to get moody if I made suggestions about things that he felt didn't or shouldn't concern me and we'd end up having pointless arguments because I made small, simple suggestions.

Mark was once asked if he had anybody that could be on hand for an extension somewhere in Shropshire and I pointed out to him that the fuel cost alone would be high. He told me to get lost and focus on the figures. In all honestly, I preferred having the outrageous Avengers-inspired behaviour to being made to feel like the crap on the bottom of his shoe.

I suppose I was hostile.

It was hard because there had been three months where I had been alone. I wanted Jen back in the house and in my life. But in that time I had mapped out a way of doing without her, which sounds harsh but it's the truth. I was always in front of the telly with a takeaway to hand, but I was also thinking about my business and what it needed. I trusted Jamie to do

115

things, but I knew he would attempt to take over the minute I was off sick (I even had a nightmare where he was driving a truck towards me and refused to stop until I handed the company over to him). My business is something that I've built up from day one. It's like a child and I need to nurture and care for it.

Mark would also not be coming to bed often.

He would get home from work, we would have dinner together and he would then set about turning the kitchen table into his own conference desk. I would head up to bed and sleep. I would then wake up in the early hours of the morning to find him asleep in front of the telly. It was odd because it was like he was living a life without me when I was right there with him. It felt surreal. I got to know what life had been like for him while I had been away and it was quite scary that he was returning to it when I was upstairs waiting for him to come to bed.

I didn't adjust overnight which was what I think bugged Jen the most.

To her it must've looked like I had wined and dined her just to shag her, get her home and carry on with the way things were already going. It wasn't like that at all but I didn't do my best to explain the situation.

I could cope with it.

I wasn't sat there thinking to myself, "Okay, he's ignoring me. I might as well ring Becca and tell her to make the spare bed up again."

Things started to get bad again.

It's not all down to me though, Doc. I know that is what I have been brought here for; to be blamed for the problems in my marriage. But I wasn't entirely to blame.

Mark's focus was not me.

I did feel as though I was something of a spare part in my home. I had returned home and my husband was carrying on his life as though I wasn't there at all.

116

Doc, you need to fully understand.

Jen had left the house and blamed me for her departure. I don't deny that I became something of a slob and just let the whole house fall away, but there was a point when I came to my senses and realised I needed to get out of the self pitying state I was in. Yes, I wanted my wife back. Yes, I wanted to return life to the way it was. But in Jen's absence I had to carry on without her. She made it feel as though I was practically single and she did that for over three months. What was I supposed to do?

Jen did break me out of a cycle but she also dropped me into a new one. I became more focused on the business than I had been and found that I love having money come in. I had let that slide and it almost became a matter of forced takeover because I'd given Jamie a lot of management responsibility when I shouldn't have done.

I was in danger of losing my business because Jamie had got a very big head in my absence, something which Jen had never spoken to me about. I was faced with sorting problems in both my professional and private life. Jamie had broken bridges with a lot of people who could put some money and work my way. Meanwhile, I'd put my marriage in jeopardy through behaviour over which I seemingly had no control.

I worked things out the opposite way around and now I think that I should have sorted the business out first, before trying to fix things with Jen. But I followed my heart – she was more important to me.

I just let it happen for a while.

I wasn't blind this time because Mark was letting me in on what was going on. He wasn't behaving weirdly, like he had before, and he was still involving me.

He was just not putting time aside for us. There would be times where I would want us to spend a day together or just cuddle up together. But he would prefer to spend time looking at spreadsheets, blueprints and costs. I didn't even bother breaking out the sexy underwear because I knew it wouldn't work on him. He was becoming very work driven.

Work became my only focus.

That was unfair to Jen but it wasn't always bad. There were times when we would work together and avoid any kind of trouble. I sometimes had to have meetings at home because the workload on the site didn't give me the opportunity to have ten minutes in my office, so my home it would have to be. And, credit where it is due, Jen helped out massively.

When Mark used to have meetings over at the house, I would try my best to work hand in hand with him rather than be selfish. I would make sure that whoever was around was made comfortable, that they had a drink. I even made sure that all Mark's paperwork was all in order.

Jen acted like a secretary at times.

I think that I abused the privilege a little bit, because I tended to have more business conferences at home rather than at the site or the clients' offices. I had a strict rule about that when I started up the business and here I was, breaking it. But I was breaking it because it was more convenient for me and easier than to break my back trying to chase things up. It's easier to ask a client to meet with you on your own turf rather than chase them to theirs and be told that they've popped out or are unavailable and will have to see you next week.

One weekend, I finally snapped.

I had organised a small party for the guys on the site.

It had been a hard slog for everybody and we had been working our arses off so I said let's go back to mine and we'll have a few drinks and enjoy the few weeks we have off. I forgot to tell Jen about this, but that wasn't what made her angry at me...

He arranged this party on our wedding anniversary.
I had planned a small intimate meal for us and, there I was, being hostess to everyone else. I wanted to throttle him.

It kind of went downhill from there.

Jen never let me forget that I had been so thoughtless and it would always lead to an argument.

I just couldn't believe that he could be so thoughtless.

He's a man, so I can forgive the forgetfulness. Every man forgets one thing throughout the day, but he was becoming more work driven and it was affecting our home life. Our house was becoming part of the job site rather than the home away from work – and it was becoming tiring.

Jen reckons that I didn't want to let go of work.

He just couldn't let go. It was like he was possessed by getting more and more money. Every day I would be hearing about new potential clients and I would see the pound signs in his eyes as he read out the numbers to me.

There is nothing wrong in working hard.

It's my own business for Christ's sake. Jen may not want to hear it, but that business has kept a roof over our heads and put food on the table. I was being made to feel like a thoughtless nobody and I was having none of it. I continued doing what I always did and kept the work going.

Things became even more work focused.

Mark would be working later and later and I was doing nothing more than clean the house and cook his dinners. I felt more like a servant than his wife.

We kept having the same argument about how I didn't pay her enough attention.

Anybody would feel the same way.

If you feel as though you're being used, then the last thing you want to do is to keep going on with your life the way that it is. So, one night I broke tradition for a change.

I was used to having dinner on the table when I got in.

119

I got home one night and found the house was empty. There was a note on the table that Jen had left for me. It said that she had gone out with a few friends and she wouldn't be back until late.

I came back from the night out and we had another blazing row.
Mark said that he wanted more warning than I gave him and he also said that it would've been nice if I had left dinner for him in the microwave rather than have him order a takeaway. I nearly went for a knife out of the kitchen drawer because he really pissed me off with that.

I've never heard Jen scream so much.
It was like she was trying to wake up a family of bats because she went ultrasonic on me.

I barely spoke to him for well over three weeks.

We conducted our lives in almost complete silence.

It's horrible. My marriage shouldn't be like that but we just didn't want to know each other. We were following different courses again.

DOCTOR'S NOTE:
"This was a very interesting session today. It seems as though Mark has been the lynchpin once again for all of the troubles happening in paradise. But you do appear to be lacking a little in understanding, Jennifer. As your husband pointed out, the business has been putting the roof over your head and stocking up the fridge. It's not easy for you to see his point of view and that is what I wish to work on for the next session. I'd like both of you to construct another letter, this time to me. Tell me what you wish to express to each other about this time."

SESSION SIXTEEN — DEAR DOCTOR

Dear Doc Foster,

I'm a businessman, or at least I would like to think that I am. I'm self employed and that brings a lot of responsibility with it. I work hard and I see the fruits of my labour when I come home to my wife. And coming home to my wife had become a problem.

She kept on getting at me because I was earning money and I was putting in the extra hours that were necessary to stop my business going into the ground. I work with some very old friends and a fair handful of them would like to take over my business. They were all jealous of how well I had built up the business from nothing and most of them wanted to do the same and branch out on their own. I get that side of things but, to start them off on that first stepping stone, they wanted to take over my business, and I don't think that my wife understands the pressure that puts me under. It's like working in a den of wolves and the minute that the leader leaves the pack, the cubs want to take over because they think that it's easy.

You've read the notes already and I feel as though I am repeating myself. So, there is my argument in a nutshell.

Mark Gardiner

Dear Doctor Foster,

I realise that I have made a lot of progress in the sessions with you in understanding that I need to be a little more thoughtful about my husband's point of view. But, in all honesty, I don't see why I should.

Through this whole period he has been completely ignorant of my feelings and just as unsympathetic as I was in the weeks after his accident; I don't see why that feeling should change now that he is completely in control of his actions. It's not difficult to put down a sheet of paper and give some attention or

121

consideration to your wife of nearly sixteen years. I wasn't asking for the world, just a couple of hours.

But no, I can't have that, can I? My husband has to make me out to be the bad guy and make everyone think that I am the one who is making things difficult in the home, when in truth it is his being completely un-thoughtful towards me that is playing a major part in that whole process. Being focused and driven by his work was never the problem. I've always known how important the business is to Mark and how he has wanted to prove to everybody that he could make it on his own. But there is a limit to how much anybody can take. He doesn't trust his pals any more because he's afraid that they will try and usurp his position. My argument is that it's Mark's company, so they will never have full control. Does he listen?

I may never be forgiven for not being the one to say it's my entire fault. But I have always put my hands up when I am wrong. I have always admitted that I could have shown a bit more sympathy and understanding during his accident and that I should have been more attentive towards his needs when I walked out on him. But I will not sit here, writing these essays, taking part in these sessions and say that it's my entire fault. I'm your wife, Mark. I'm not a maid, a secretary, or one of your site workers, here to issue orders to. You want to be all about your work. Fine, take me out of the equation, because it's all you have done recently.

Yours, Jennifer Gardiner

DOCTOR'S NOTE:

"Both of you have expressed your points of view quite clearly and I think that something positive needs to come from that. Mark, maybe you could take your wife's feelings into consideration a little more and leave work at work. Jennifer, maybe you could tell your husband directly what it is you want so that he fully is aware and then the friction between the pair of you can be avoided. Next session, I think that we will have a discussion regarding the two of you and where the emotional levels are at the moment. Can you both communicate reasonably?"

OPEN COMMUNICATION TRANSCRIPT
Session One with Dr L Foster

DR FOSTER

Well, we've made some excellent progress in the last few weeks and this is the reason that I have asked us to begin with these open communication sessions. Mark, you have become more open and Jennifer you have become very honest about your insensitivity towards your husband. The point of these open communication sessions is to try and get a feel for where we go next in your counselling. First, I would like to assess what has brought you to these sessions.

MARK

Jen made me. Pure and simple.

JENNIFER

I did not. All I said was that we needed help to put our marriage back on track. It's not my fault that you're too pig headed to realise that I want to help us stay together. At least I'm making an effort. All you want to do is be argumentative and closed off.

DR FOSTER

Back to my original point; what was it that made you both seek a counsellor?

JENNIFER

It's like I put in the journal entries; Mark had become too work driven and it was driving me mad. I felt that I was a stranger in my own marriage and he did nothing to remedy that.

MARK

And she was never letting me forget it. All I do is go out and work my arse off. Then I come home and get it in the neck because she feels that I'm ignoring her. I can't win, Doc. I'm getting knives in the jugular wherever I turn.

JENNIFER

You have ignored me, Mark! You've been selfish. You've been arrogant. You've been dismissive and you've treated me like a valet and a secretary. I'm not your wife any more!

MARK

Really? That was a quick divorce.

JENNIFER

Very funny. Instead of making crap jokes, why don't you put your side across? Seeing as how you think I'm wrong all the time.

MARK

All I was doing was trying to keep the business going. It's my business and I wanted it to keep being successful. Not that my wife can see that, Doc. All she sees is someone horrible that doesn't know what it means to love his wife and try to keep the roof over her head.

JENNIFER

I can see the hard work that you put in, but it's only business that you think about. When was the last time that you ever wanted to do something with me? When was the last time that we got to spend some quality time together as a couple?

MARK

We have time together.

JENNIFER

Sleeping together doesn't count.

DR FOSTER
Okay, let's calm it down a second. Jennifer, how would you define 'time together'?

JENNIFER
Easy, take him away from all the paperwork and let his mates down there do their job without him breathing down their necks. Let everyone that you are paying to do a job get on with it and remember that you have a wife at home who wants to see you and spend some time with you. Let your workers do some work.

MARK
I can't do that.

DR FOSTER
Why not, Mark?

JENNIFER
He doesn't want to.

MARK
That's not true.

JENNIFER
It is true. You think nothing about me and my feelings. It's always about the bloody business and I'm getting sick of it.

MARK
Really? Going to walk out of the house again, are you?

JENNIFER
Don't tempt me!

DR FOSTER
Mark, what is the reason that you have been so work driven lately?

125

MARK
I can't say.

JENNIFER
He doesn't love me anymore, that's the reason.

MARK
Get off my case, Jen!

JENNIFER
You see?

DR FOSTER
Mark, I think the only proper resolution we will ever have is if you tell us why you are being so devoted to your work recently because it has put a strain on your marriage.

MARK
We nearly went bankrupt. When I built up the business I used a lot of personal capital to set it up and a part of that was the house. When Jamie was left in charge, he got sloppy. He didn't understand the system for the books and ended nearly writing off some of my investments. So he brought in outsiders to go over the books and was given advice on how to make my company into a real successful business by merging with a conglomerate. In doing so he nearly bought into a company that would've liquidated any assets that we had.

(For the benefit of the notes, Jennifer was somewhat in a state of shock.)

DR FOSTER
Go on, Mark.

MARK

It was a shambles. I asked Jamie to take the helm of the company, oversee the constructions and make sure that we all got to the same point on time. Instead, he tried to play company manager and tied me up in deadlock litigation. I've only just been able to sort out my half of the bills, let alone pay the mortgage. Thanks to him I'm nearly over £5,000 in debt to the middle men that he hired to oversee the accounts.

JENNIFER

Why didn't you tell me this?

MARK

I didn't want to admit defeat. It's my company and I can bail it out of the shit. I proved that I can make it to my dad and I can prove it to myself.

JENNIFER

So, I don't fit into any of this, then?

MARK

It's all about you! Everything that I have done to get out of this mess has been for you!

JENNIFER

If you had any consideration or thought towards me you would've told me about it from day one. You know how much help I have given to you with the books. We could've sat down together and made a proper plan and got out of the mess just as quickly – or quicker – than you could on your own. You and your bloody pride.

MARK

And then what, Jen? What would you do? All this happened during your three months away from the house. I can't afford to get someone to bail me out all the time and I will not be made to admit that I couldn't take it. You never have any faith in me.

JENNIFER

How can I when you're so secretive? This has gone on for months and you have not said anything to me.

MARK

I knew that you would be judgemental, that's why. From day one, you told me that I shouldn't have trusted Jamie to take the reins because you didn't trust him.

JENNIFER

Was I wrong?

MARK

No. You were right. But if you hadn't walked out on me after the accident then I wouldn't have put him in that position.

JENNIFER

Oh, so now it's my fault?

MARK

Yes. It is your fault. You have no idea how much pain you put me through. I wasn't sleeping in our bed because I was missing you so much. I was staring at our wedding picture wanting you to come back to me and wondering what the hell made you leave me. And on top of it all, I couldn't ask for your help to sort out the business.

JENNIFER

Babe, calm down...

MARK

Don't try to sweet talk me. You're the one that brought me to these counselling sessions and each time you have made me think that I'm the one with a problem. Well here are the facts, Jen. I've been through hell after being hit with a wrecking ball whilst trying to have a crap in a portable toilet. I've put my own company in a mess because I placed a wannabe god in my place in the captain's chair. I've had you throw every problem in our marriage at me and now you want me to keep admitting that you're always right?

DR FOSTER
Mark, please calm yourself.

MARK
Don't you start, Doc. I've felt like a kid in detention with all your journal notes and one-on-one sessions. I've had enough of everyone trying to tell me that I'm in the wrong. When is it my turn to be right?

(For the benefit of the notes, Mark stormed out of the office)

END OF OPEN COMMUNICATION SESSION.

DOCTOR'S NOTE:
"This session has shed a lot of light on the issues that have built up since Mark's accident. Mark has been put in the position of the underdog, under his wife's heels, and I think that if we had not progressed to the open communication sessions this would have gone unspoken. I also think that there may be a small amount of bitterness about not being chased himself during the initial break-up in the marital home and having no proof of worth within the relationship. In turn, Jennifer seemed to turn a corner in her outlook thanks to the session itself and (after Mark had stormed out) she now realises that things are not always what they seem. The next one-to-one session with the couple has been scheduled and I have asked for the journals to continue."

SESSION SEVENTEEN

Mark has left home this time.
He left me a note to say that he would be at Jamie's if I needed to reach
him. I find that ironic. When he needed a shoulder to cry on, he's gone to the
person that has caused him so much grief, when that shoulder should have been
mine. I think I fucked this up a little bit.

Doc, I need to thank you.

Talking does help a lot. I went round to Jamie's and I had it out with him. I told him that I thought he was an absolute twat for placing my company into the hands of mercenaries that were going to turn it into slipshod operation that would exist under a single umbrella and be filled with staff that wouldn't know one end of a brick from the other.

I also told him off for thinking that he my asking him to cover for me with the day-to-day running of the business gave him power to make changes without recourse to me. He was not full-time chairman; he was the caretaker. I was off work due to very personal circumstances and he knew of this. It was bad of him to take advantage of that in the way that he did and communicated this while landing a bunch of fives right on his jaw.

I then informed him that I had left home. I arrived on his door with a suitcase and told him that he better take me in for a few nights or he could kiss his employment goodbye. He agreed to take me in and I made sure that Jen knew where I was. Not that it would matter, seeing as my feelings mean nothing in her eyes.

So all I can do now is thank you, Doc. Having that one-to-one as we did really did get me in touch with the anger I was feeling towards Jamie. I think that after this incident the two of us will soon be back on a firm footing.

I tried ringing him but didn't get anywhere.

I'm not speaking to Jen right now.

That open communication session let me know exactly where I stand in the scheme of things. I'm not going to be a punch bag every time my wife – my *wife*, Doc – needs one. I know that it is meant to be that way and that the wedding vows were to love, honour and obey, but I didn't recite the vows of 'be a mug, take the blame for everything and be walked over'.

It's hard to believe that there was a time when Jen was the voice of reason. It's only since I had my accident that she became so selfish. Everything needs to be about her and her feelings. Was she the one that got launched into space whilst sitting on a portable loo? Was she having bouts of memory loss? Was she the one that was acting the fool and forgetting about it as though she had been hypnotised? No, it was all me.

I guess he'll have to stay mad at me for a little bit.

I've never seen him so angry at me. Maybe he's right. Maybe I did offload onto him a little bit but I didn't mean for it to spiral out of control. I did see things from his side. I was just never vocal about the whole thing. I was vocal about how he was making me feel. I was vocal about how he was keeping his distance. I was vocal about how he was not interested in me any more.

But now I think I'm finally seeing things from his side of the coin. He's left me here all alone this time. I never knew how quiet it could be around this place without the television on. It's odd because I seem to be doing the same things that he described at the counselling session the other day. I'm sat in his chair, staring at our wedding picture on the wall and thinking how gorgeous Mark looked on that day. I'm starting to not want to go to bed because I know that he's not going to be there to put his arm round me in the middle of the night. He's right. I have put him through some pain.

I think the reason that he kept me in the dark with everything was that he didn't want me to leave again. He had no idea as to why I left the last time and I really wish that I had told him the reason that I stormed out of the house without telling him. He must've been driven crazy by that. But now I know that he was trying to save the business... Well, that completely puts things into a different perspective.

Would I have left the house again if he had told me...? I don't think that I can answer that one.

131

The boot is on the other foot now, Doc.

Let's see how she likes being made to feel like the marriage wrecker.

DOCTOR'S NOTE:

"There are major feelings of reflection here and I can see that the two of you are now in juxtapositions with each other. Mark, you have become a lot more open since the last meeting as you feel that you have finally been given a chance to air your feelings on the whole situation. This is very positive and it is allowing you to finally express what you have been holding back. It has also made you take a somewhat irrational action to make your point be known. While this factor may not be completely healthy, it is good to know that you are expressing yourself. Jennifer, you are seeing things on the opposite side of the coin and are showing a willingness to take the responsibility for your actions in this matter. This is excellent, as the sessions began with you attempting to understand where Mark was coming from in terms of behaviour, and, now that you are going through the same process that he had to work through, it is giving you an objective perspective. The one thing that the two of you have lacked is the ability to communicate, and this is vital to a resolution. Mark has left the marital home in the same way that Jennifer left previously. For the next session, let us try to find a way forward."

SESSION EIGHTEEN

Jamie has been a very good friend recently.

He's been letting me get on with things the way they should be done and has been careful not to take on anything I've not asked him to do (and especially nothing on a management level). He has however taken a few messages from Jen over the past week. I admit that I shouldn't still be angry with her, but I am.

I can't put it into words, Doc. As much as I love her and as much as I miss being with her, I cannot go back if I know that we are going to be at loggerheads all the time. It was never like that in the beginning; it's only been since the accident. I've come to curse that accident – I was its first victim; the second was my marriage. My wife has gone from being someone that I can talk to and turned into someone that I can barely stand the sight of. That isn't right.

I've been missing Mark so much.

I've left messages with Jamie to try and get him to contact me but I've had no luck. If only Mark would ring me. We could sort this if he would just think for a moment and try. I'm trying, for God's sake.

I know that I should ring her.

I know that I should be a bigger man.

I know that she wants things sorted.

All I have to do is pick up the phone.

With everything that has gone on since we got together, my first instinct is to always ring Jen. She's my wife. She is my first port of call for anything. But it's not been that way for us for a while now. Ever since my accident (I sound like a bloody broken record!), it's been different. It reads like a shopping list; I've been left alone in my own home, my wife wouldn't talk to me, we then get back together, I try my best to make the money for us to live on and she's still not happy, and we split for a second time. What do I have to do, Doc?

I did hear one of the voice messages she left earlier this week. It was nice to hear her voice and she was asking if we can put all of this behind us and start fresh. In all honesty, Doc, I'm not sure I can. I don't know if I'm able to go back to things as they were, because now I have spoken up about how I feel, it all keeps playing around in my head. It puts me at a disadvantage in my own marriage and I hate it. Jen is the love of my life and we were in conflict so much because I was trying to do what was right for us. At least I thought that I was doing the right thing for us. You see, Doc? There I go again with the feelings of being bullied and put upon.

Am I making something out of nothing?

DOCTOR'S NOTE:
"You raise an interesting question, Mark. But it appears that you want Jennifer to do all of the work in getting you back together. You're putting her in the same position that she put you in when she left you. Although I can see where you're coming from, it does seem that you are point scoring. You seem to be trying to find out how dedicated she is to you, which is not always the best course of action to take."

Oh really, Doc?

And where in your medical journals and dictionaries does it say that you have to be right in everything? You've got me here writing in a journal notebook like a child doing homework and you're telling me that I am point scoring. Who the hell do you think you are?

You wait until it's your turn and your partner, the person you love with your whole soul, rips your heart out and walks out of the house without telling you why. You wait until *you* have to spend months sleeping alone in a cold house in front of the telly every night because your wife won't pick up the phone. *You* wait until you go about your routine of working and making sure that every bill is paid only to find out that what you're doing is never good enough for *your* partner.

Then you can tell me when it's wrong to point score.

DOCTOR'S NOTE:

"Mark; let's not make this a personal issue. I am here to help you, and sometimes my comments might seem hurtful, but your defensive, emotional response suggests that I have hit a nerve. I think you realise, deep down, that there is perhaps some truth to my suggestion. Regardless, it has allowed you to share some more feelings that you've kept under wraps. Keep going with that. For the next session, I want each of you to construct another letter to the other, explaining your feelings. Be really expressive and honest with each other."

SESSION NINETEEN — THE LETTERS

To Jennifer,

I apologise for not answering your many messages. I have been busy keeping the business afloat and the roof over your head – a roof that I should still be living under and would be if you could see that all the work I am doing is for us both. If you had only opened your eyes, or just let me get on with it, then maybe I would have let you in on things. Instead, you kept getting at me, whatever I was doing.

Where am I going wrong, Jen? What is it? Was it something I said? Was it something that I did? You don't talk to me about things. It's been that way for a while, but I didn't want to rock the boat by speaking up about it. I just put it out of my mind and told myself that it was just my imagination. But I've had enough of having to read between the lines to find out what the problem is. You have become as unpredictable as an English summer. The smallest things can change your mood and I was always the one that would be getting it in the neck. All I was doing was going about my routine of working so that we could live comfortably.

And since when has it been a problem that I work? You were never bothered by it before, so why does it bother you now? I apologise if I seem to be prioritising towards work, but the mortgage won't pay itself. It does take two incomes to keep things flowing (unless the government has changed its policies towards the workers) and I have been the one that has taken the flack for picking up the slack and being the main provider to the table. Should I be feeling bad about that? I'm not going to feel bad about it. I'm an independent businessman and the company is thriving thanks to the hard work that I've put into it since wresting control back from Jamie. I would prefer you to be celebrating my success with me, but it's obviously a bone of contention with you, even now.

What has happened to us? We used to be so solid. I hold my hands up to the things that are my fault, but I'm not responsible for what has happened to us recently. I admit that I am guilty for being work driven but that is all I am guilty of.

Let's sort this out. You're my wife and we should be together. But I will only be willing to talk when you stop placing the blame for everything onto me. It's not fair, especially when I am only trying to do right by you.

Love, Mark xx

To Mark,

I want you to come home. The bed is lonely without you and I'm missing you being around the house. I realise that it was because of me that you to walked out of the house, and I guess that I deserved it to happen to me after what happened before. But there were reasons behind my actions and I need you to take them into consideration.

I've never lied to you in our whole marriage or our life together, but I have to be honest and say that there are times when I feel that you do not appreciate me, in particular your recent behaviour regarding our relationship. It's almost as if, in your eyes, I do not exist. When I moved back in, I thought that things would return to some kind of normality, and they did for a short while. I appreciate that you have to keep the business going and keep the funds coming in, as you always tell me. But I'm your wife. Doesn't that count for anything? Do I not matter at all?

I do accept responsibility for getting at you a lot recently. I apologise to you for this. But my reason for it is something that I need you to understand. I feel as though you have been neglecting me, especially on the night of our anniversary; you filled the house with people that you work with when I had plans for us to spend an intimate evening together. Did you consider my feelings in that matter? You didn't even talk to me about it beforehand? And then any time that I try and spend with you, it always ends up with you sitting at the kitchen table, attending to the business.

I have taken a back seat to everything, with very little complaint. But for God's sake, Mark, I want to spend some time where it is just us. Please, come home, and we can sort all this out.

Love you, Jennifer xxx

DOCTOR'S NOTE:

"There is a lot of raw emotion in both of these letters. What you both have said to each other demonstrates a communication breakdown. A marriage cannot succeed without communication. In each of our sessions together, you have managed to achieve the goals set, but in this particular case, you have fallen a little short. You have both embraced change, but independently; the two of you have not changed anything together. For the next session, go away and don't talk to each other for a week. See what the end result is. Do you feel differently when you do not contact each other? Is there ground to build on if there is an enforced distance?"

SESSION TWENTY

God, I want to stop writing in this bloody thing. It's like being back at school and handing in your work for marking by the teacher.

Before you ask, Doc, no I have not spoken to Jen at all this week. And yes, it has been interesting. I've become used to the phone ringing as soon as I get through the door from work. It was weird not hearing it go off as I was shaving each morning. I'll give my wife credit in that she was determined and punctual in the times that she would call me. It has been weird though.

It's been unusual to not have any contact with Mark.
I have wanted to pick up the phone and speak to him. To hear his voice always seemed to make the day go okay for me. But, in the current state of our relationship, it's making me feel both separate from him alongside wanting to be near him.

It's unreal.

I would get into Jamie's and the first thing I would hear would be my mobile going off. I would then have an hour long session of dancing to my ringtone due to Jen ringing at least thirty times. I never answered because all we would discuss would be when I was coming home. I didn't want that discussion because I'm still not ready to go home. I'm still unsure as to whether I'm going to be hugged or yelled at the minute that I get through my own front door. Things shouldn't be like that.

I've been visiting the pub a little more frequently too. It's been a nice release not to have Jen say that I can or can't do things like that. She only started to mind recently, but I work hard and I deserve that sort of time to myself. Not only that, but I can also look at other women without being given a guilt trip by Jen. In the pub, there are many women about and I can just be around them without feeling Jen's eyes burn into the back of my head. I like women, it's not a crime. Anyway, it never goes beyond looking

139

because I have married the most gorgeous woman on the planet – my wedding ring is a testament to that. But it's nice to not get the full force of Jen's jealousy for a change, particularly with all the other hassles that I have to deal with.

I've seen a lot of my family in this past week.

It's been really lovely and everyone is supportive that Mark and I will resolve our differences. So am I, if I'm really honest. I've known him for a long while and I know how his mind works. But I don't want to wait forever. I would love it if he just came through the door and we had the chance to sit down and talk everything through.

But my mum has advised me to let things go at the pace suggested by you, Doctor Foster. Looking at the amount of calls that I placed in Mark's direction has shown me that I was a little pushy in my attempts to get my own husband to just talk to me.

My dad has also pointed out to me that things always work out if the love is strong enough. My parents are good like that, very sage and wise. But I am missing my husband. It's different now that I know that I was the one that drove him crazy this time around. I know exactly how he is feeling and that is something that I did not want to put upon him.

It still feels odd.

Jen always rings me. She never fails. I guess that I've become so used to having her call me that it's been odd to have her not ring me. I find it strange how I should be thinking about that now, having just written this section after getting back from another pub session. I'm not drunk, but I've had the freedom in which to drink. I feel more relaxed and it's because I'm not in contact with my wife. And that is something that I never thought that I would say. But in truth I'm only saying it because I am partly still angry at feeling like an argumentative punch bag. I'm bound to feel different when I don't have someone suggesting that every single problem is my fault.

I think that I will keep contact with Mark restricted.
Not forever, but until he is ready to talk to me properly.

DOCTOR'S NOTE:

"There have been some wonderful insights from these journal entries. Both of you have taken the lack of contact in different ways; Mark has struggled with the normality of regularly hearing from his wife being taken from him but he has enjoyed a small amount of personal freedom that was not being offered to him in his marriage. Meanwhile, Jennifer has enjoyed not being so forceful in her attempts to establish the contact and has had to accept being patient. From these entries in particular, it is clear that contact should be re-established, but that the experiences of the last week can perhaps add a fresh dynamic to your interaction. For the next session, we will have another open communication hour in which we will tackle this current period of communication between the two of you and we will see whether we can arrive at a possible solution."

OPEN COMMUNICATION TRANSCRIPT
Session Two with Dr L Foster

DR FOSTER
Welcome again, Mark and Jennifer.
Now, in recent sessions we have been looking at how things have turned full circle due to Mark leaving the house.

MARK
I didn't have much choice. I was being hounded like a criminal.

JENNIFER
I never hounded you. I just wanted to spend some time with you. Forgive me for wanting to enjoy something that we call our marriage. It does involve the two of us, you know?

DR FOSTER
If I could interject?
Now, the point of this session is to properly assess where things are now for the two of you. At the start of our journey together, you were both here due to overburdening circumstances. Mark had gone through a terrible ordeal and the journey back from that had to be made. But now we've become stuck in a phase of constant arguing and distance.

MARK
The distance is down to her.

JENNIFER
You walked out of the house.

MARK
I followed your example.

DR FOSTER
Be that as it may, what I would like for us to do now is to try and reach
a resolution for the two of you.

MARK
No chance.

JENNIFER
Why are you being so difficult?

MARK
I'm still waiting for an apology. I'm waiting for several apologies, in
fact.

JENNIFER
So, you've done nothing wrong, like always?

MARK
You started this.

JENNIFER
No, I didn't. You did. You walked out on me.

MARK
I didn't the first time round.

DR FOSTER
Hold on! This circular argument is helping neither of you. Let's focus
on the here and now.

MARK
Alright, I'm here, and I want an apology – now.

143

JENNIFER
You see what I have to put up with, Doctor Foster? He ignores every message I send him, he never listens to me, and he keeps attacking me when I try to sort things out. He is being totally unreasonable

DR FOSTER
Does Jennifer have a point, Mark?

(For the benefit of the notes, Mark remained silent)

JENNIFER
Finally, he admits that I'm right.

MARK
I admit nothing. All I will say is that in the last God knows how many weeks, I have been made to feel like an ant under your shoe. You've made my efforts to keep a business going seem stupid, you've made it seem as though I have been inattentive towards you, and have made me out to be argumentative. I can't even go out for a quick drink after work because you lay down the law.

JENNIFER
You've been all those things.

MARK
What do you want? What do you want me to say, Jen? Okay, hands up, I admit to you here and now in front of our therapist that I focused too much on work. But I only did it because I felt neglected by you.

JENNIFER
How did I neglect you?

MARK
How many times did I ask you to go 50/50 with me so that everything would get done quicker? How many times did I ask you to keep the books

in check so I knew what was what? How many times did I tell you that I had made plans for us?

JENNIFER
You never made plans for us.

MARK
For our anniversary, I planned to take you to dinner in the place I proposed to you. For your last birthday I tried to organise a spa weekend for you to go to that you turned down in favour of a weekend with your sister. And the week before I left the house I tried to organise a dinner for two.

JENNIFER
I don't remember that.

MARK
You played the message left by the office?

JENNIFER
That was a message from Jamie saying that the materials you ordered had been put in place and needed to be dealt with immediately.

MARK
That was me making the reservation for that night.

JENNIFER
You did nothing that weekend I was with Rebecca.

MARK
How do you think Rebecca secured a hotel reservation for two nights at such short notice? And where did she get the £800 for the weekend from?

JENNIFER
She told me that she won on a scratch card.

MARK

She's never gambled in her life. She vowed only to gamble if she ever got a holiday to Las Vegas, which will never happen because she spends any money she makes like water. Do you not know your own sister?

JENNIFER

You never plan anything for our anniversaries.

MARK

I thought it would be nice to surprise you. I am capable of doing that, you know.

(For the benefit of the notes, Jennifer remained silent and a little subdued. Mark then got a little agitated after these admissions and left the room.)

END OF OPEN COMMUNICATION SESSION.

DOCTOR'S NOTE:

"This was a very illuminating session, especially for Jennifer. Once Mark had left the room, she admitted to me that she may have been too rigid in her critique of her husband. You made very good progress today, Mark. You opened up completely in this particular session and your vulnerability may have gone a great way in helping repair your marriage. For the next session we will return to the journals and focus on the aftermath of this session. Leave them for two weeks and then return to them. Write about the events that occurred between you after your second open communication session."

SESSION TWENTY-ONE

I got thinking after the last face-to-face session.

I had been very unfair on Mark since the accident. I didn't mean to be, but the way that things were going between us made me feel as though I was becoming an outcast in my own marriage. I felt that my feelings were being discarded and the one thing that nobody wants to feel in a relationship is ignored and lonely. What I overlooked was that this was exactly how my husband felt, too, but that was because we never ever spoke about it.

Over the last two weeks I've avoided all contact with him. I think he needed some breathing space and time to think. In all honesty, we both did. It has allowed me to realise that Mark could have been experiencing the same problems and feelings of inadequacy that I was going through.

Two weeks of not hearing from Jen has been very weird.

The last session was interesting. I had no idea that I was going to be so forward. I still have no idea what happened. I came to the meeting all prepared to be tense and argumentative with my wife and all of a sudden I ended up baring my soul. I had wanted to say everything to Jen for a long time but I didn't want to rock the boat. She had only just come back home and I didn't want to make her leave again. I don't honestly think that I made her leave the last time. I think that my behaviour simply scared her. I can understand that now. Time has proved that I wasn't crazy and that I was genuinely suffering.

But ever since she came back we haven't fully connected with each other. I hate that. She is the sexiest woman in the world and I am married to her. I still take great pride in that. But I haven't heard from her or bothered to contact her in two weeks. It sounds harsh, but, in all honesty, Doc, I have no starting place. I have run dry of ideas that will reassure her of my love. I think it's all down to the fact that I know that is what she wants. She wants me to run after her and keep chasing until she is ready to listen. She wants me to keep banging down the doors that she keeps closing on me.

I don't honestly think that I *can* keep chasing her. It sounds horrible. I love my wife to death, but this is getting too much. I feel as though my feelings on the subject are being ignored and once again I am the one who has to clean up a mess that I am not completely responsible for.

Okay, where the hell did that come from?

I sent Mark a message, out of the blue.

I felt that I needed to make some amends and start fresh, for my own peace of mind. Mark didn't reply for a few days. It drove me crazy. I wanted more than anything to start being the chaser in all of this, which sounds unusual considering that I wanted that from him in the first place. But seeing the way he became so open and honest in that face-to-face opened my eyes to the fact that he does take things on board.

Out of the blue, Jen messaged me.

It was great to hear from her considering the fortnight's silence. I looked at it and thought to myself that I'm in a silent marriage! It's crazy. The message just said whether I felt like meeting and having a long and proper talk to sort out our marriage. I had to think a bit. Jen may have made me feel bad about things going wrong and may have called me everything under the sun, but she is my wife – and I've missed her. If I didn't love her and want to be with her, then we'd be facing the dreaded 'D' word. I thought about everything that she means to me and what it is about her that makes me love her; the usual mushy stuff that all men think about, but cannot bear to admit. My mind was made up. We had to meet and sort everything out, so I messaged back with my agreement.

Mark told me that he wanted to sort things, but it wasn't enough for me.

I remembered how good he made me feel by pulling out all of the stops when our first problems began. I wanted to do the same thing for him, too. If I wanted to make things completely right, then I needed to go all out and so I went shopping.

Things went silent for a little bit.

I really tried to get it right.
I thought about how Mark had gone about things and I went through
every shop that was in town. I looked for the right outfit and I decided to go
with the idea of a romantic meal. It had worked for me before, when Mark got
it absolutely right.
Having just the meal on its own seemed a bit dull, so I went around the
town again to look for the right kind of movie to set the mood. It was harder
than I expected to find one to suit the reunion I'd got in mind for Mark. For
some strange reason, I found myself wandering into the music shop.
Even though VHS is as dead as a dodo, this small, independent music shop
still had a few stacks of tapes to clear, beneath a sign declaring "VHS at Bargain
Prices". As we still have our old player (and even a backup player in the attic for
the day when the current one stops working), I took a look at the section. And
along the top shelf I saw something that caused a strange sensation, a mixture of
a chill and elation. It was a video of The Avengers – and it gave me an idea.

Jen texted me and said to watch out for an invitation.
I remember the way that I'd done things before and wondered whether
she may be thinking along the same lines. I could've been wrong but I was
hopeful that something positive would come from it all. Everyone has to
hope, don't they, Doc?
I'll be honest, I'm quite excited about it.

The plan then came to me.
I don't know why, but I bought that tape of The Avengers. If anything, I
liked the pink cover and the corny title of the cassette, The M Appeal Collection.
Whoever thought of that was clever, playing on the name of Steed's partner.
Anyway, I read the list of episodes it contained, including the one about the
treasure hunt that I'd already seen, but the other ones I had never heard of
before. I started to watch the tape and it immediately brought back the feelings I
had about Mark's accident. I hate how sometimes I can't take anything in and
get distracted by random thoughts, but at least I was watching the show that he
had used to win me back before.

The first one I saw was a black and white. It was an interesting one that involved dressing up and play acting, all set in a bizarre gentleman's club called Hellfire.

DOCTOR'S NOTE:
The Avengers – A TOUCH OF BRIMSTONE (1965)
"Practical jokes are befalling important individuals, often with fatal consequences. In finding out why, Steed and Mrs Peel connect the incidents to an authentic recreation of the infamous Hellfire Club…"

I liked the outfit that Mrs Peel wore.

I knew immediately that Mark would love to see me in an outfit like that, but there was no way that I'd wear a spiked collar. It would be too embarrassing to explain to others if we got intimate and something went wrong! I then watched the treasure hunt episode, which of course Mark had played out when out of control.

The last episode was really spooky, chilling at times. It centred on Mrs Peel visiting a house where she kept leaving and entering the same room – the whole building was a machine.

DOCTOR'S NOTE:
The Avengers – THE HOUSE THAT JACK BUILT (1966)
"Mrs Peel is bequeathed a house that appears to be a beautiful and lovely inheritance. But it appears that her Uncle Jack has a family connection that is set to have deadly results…"

But the whole thing then came together.

If Mark could use The Avengers to win me around, then I was going to do the same for him. I wanted to prove to my husband that our marriage was still worth everything to me. I wanted to make an event of it, so I went out and found somewhere that did specialised invitations for parties. I chose the one with the most elaborate, fancy design. I sent Mark the invitation with a date and time. I wasted no time in putting the rest of my Avengers Reunion plan into motion.

A friend of Jen's turned up at the job site and handed over a small, sealed envelope.

I opened it and saw that it was an invitation card, nicely decorated. From the look of the invite she was being playful. It looked beautiful, like she had designed it by hand. The instructions came with a small map with crosses on it. It looked like we were to act out something from a late 1960s spy movie – I seemed to be a contact being given coded information that I had to follow as if my life depended on it. It seemed a lot of fun.

I decided to use all three episodes of The Avengers that I had seen. I put the treasure hunt episode into action first.

I followed the instructions on the map, and I found myself heading in the direction of the job site. I saw Jamie there and the first thing that he said to me was that I needed to follow the clue on the reverse side of the invitation. I found the clue that Jen had left for me and wound up looking for the red safe deposit box that is kept in the office safe. I still had my keys on me so I opened it. There was another card inside. As you guessed it, Doc, there were more directions to follow, so I left the job site quickly.

I had no idea where the hell I was going. The instructions were quite clear and told me that I would need to find "Mr Smith's hammer". I was more confused than ever until I saw on the side of the road one of my chippies, Harry Smith, who was gesturing towards me as if hailing a cab. I pulled over and asked him if he wanted a ride somewhere, as long as it wasn't far from my destination. All he did was hand me a hammer and another instruction card. He then told me to hit the direct centre of the card with the hammer and it would reveal something in the indentation.

Doc, I'm not normally slow on the uptake but I had to admit that I thought this was completely wild and crazy. I did as instructed and found that the circle part of the hammer had been covered in something red. I think that Jen had used her lipstick on it. I hit the centre of the card and a

151

red ring was all that I was left with. I turned the card over and realised that I had hit the wrong side. Fortunately there was more lipstick on the hammer so i did it again. It was a really small map but I could read that it was in the directions that I had been following on the previous card.

I followed the instructions on the new card, which led to Jen's favourite restaurant.

I had been here before with Jen but she had taken me around the long way. I prefer to take very direct routes when I drive but this one had me taking in villages and back streets. She obviously wanted to keep the mystery part of the evening going for a while.

I arrived first and was told that the reservation was for two, and we would be seated in a private room in the back. When I entered I found a red rose on the table and two candles. I then discovered that the waiter was going to be with us for the whole night and I knew that the money side of things was not going to be looked at until much later.

I used the Hellfire episode for my choice of outfit.

I was at the table waiting for Jen.

I was quite nervous. I still don't know if this was a good or a bad thing. Should you be nervous about seeing your wife? We were in a pretty rocky state, but it looked like we were re-connecting and following some sort of a plan that would have us bonking like two teenagers on a first date. Anyway, Jen then entered the restaurant. I nearly fainted when she entered the room.

I chose a black velvet halter neck dress, which opened at the cleavage, and had a very short skirt which hugged the figure a little. At least I didn't have the underwire of a bra digging into my ribcage all night! I had never worn anything like this before. I normally went for knee length dresses, but I was determined to win my husband back and this was one way in which to do it. I have to be honest and say that I felt sexy. There are times when you go all out to impress your partner and it's always a 50/50 as to how the night will turn out based on the outfit. But if I was feeling this way about it, I was certain that this part of the scheme was going to be a success.

Jen was in the sexiest outfit I've ever seen her in.

I was reminded that night of just how lucky I am. She was hot, Doc. I couldn't speak.

Mark's jaw dropped as I walked in, which was the reaction I was hoping for.

His eyes were glued to me, I could feel it. It was nice to have that sort of attention from him after so long. Even when we sat down to eat, his eyes were burning into me. I loved it because it felt like all those years ago in P.E. at school, when Mark's eyes would be glued to my bum throughout each lesson. He would pretend he wasn't looking, to look macho in front of his friends, but I knew what he was doing. He had the same stare now as he did back then and I knew that he was thinking hard about how things would go after the meal. But, as before, he was the perfect gentleman.

We had a really nice dinner.

But it felt different. From the moment that we sat at that table, there was no tension at all between us. It was like all the confessions we made in our journals and all the meetings we'd had were non-existent.

It was a lovely meal.

I seemed to be able to connect with Mark in a way that I'd not been able to for a while. All the turmoil of the last few months just washed away from us. We didn't say one thing that pressed those buttons of aggravation. It was just us. The rest of the room, the world, fell away to leave me in the moment with the greatest man I've ever known.

She had organised everything perfectly.

She made me feel as though I was the only person in her world. Considering how up and down we both had been with each other, and how hostile I had sometimes been during the counselling sessions (yes, Doc, I admit it!), none of that mattered.

We had a big meal, though. Jen had apparently paid for everything in advance, which shocked me because normally I would always insist on paying. My wife was full of surprises for me on that night.

When we had finished dessert, I put the last part of the plan into action.

Knowing Mark as I do, I was sure that seeing me in my outfit would be making his blood pump and his eyes bulge from their sockets. And I cannot deny that there was a specific reason why I chose to wear an outfit that accentuated my cleavage and allowed my husband to see what he had been missing. I think you can guess what I was working towards, Doctor Foster...

After the meal, Jen insisted we go home.

I hadn't been back to our house for a few weeks, but she was looking so delicious that I didn't want to say no. I walked her to the door and we flirtatiously played with words as she got the key out.

Once I got him into that house, he was all mine.

We were all over each other. I hadn't kissed Mark in ages and it was so exhilarating. I then led him up to the bedroom and kept him in there. I wanted to remind him of how he made me feel like I was the only woman in his life and I wanted to let him know that he was the only man I wanted.

Jen made me sit on the bed for what seemed like ages.

I went back to the Hellfire episode for the last part of the night.

I remember the outfit that Mrs Peel wore and I thought that Mark would love to see me in something similar, so I went shopping and found an unusual garment that met the requirements. It was a black velvet style corset that hugged the figure beautifully and zipped up at the front rather than tied up. It went up to the cleavage and it thrust my boobs so far forward that they could knock a man's eyes out at forty paces. The only piece that I needed to complete the outfit was something that I'd always had and always had Mark melting.

She then came back in.

Doc, I nearly exploded. She was wearing this gorgeous outfit that looked like a cross between a swimming costume and a thong! How the hell could I resist?

I wasn't wearing the corset for very long, I remember.

154

The sex that followed was incredible, special, the best I've ever had, and I know that I've already said that more than once in these notes! Jen is an amazing woman, so sensual and responsive – and she's all mine.

I may have had suspicions that the purpose of the evening was to get me back home, but she did show me exactly what I was missing. So, after we had our bed session, we managed to talk things through.

Mark has agreed to come back home.

This was the ultimate goal, but it was the best chance we had to really sort things out between us. It wasn't underhand and I'm feeling quite proud that it worked. All sex aside, we really did manage to reconnect and talk things through again, which was another target. It didn't feel right that progress was only hyappening in the sessions we were having with you, Doctor Foster. It may sound like a cliché, but The Avengers has, in some way, saved my marriage again.

DOCTOR'S NOTE:

"We have definitely reached a breakthrough. Jennifer you have executed a plan that could have backfired, but you stuck to it. Mark, you have opened up and allowed your aggressive emotions to be put at bay and have allowed your mind to opened up to the possibilities of further communication. The individual sessions have dealt with all the separate sides and individual issues of your problems and I think that the suggestion of the open communication sessions allowed the two of you to reconnect as a couple and gave the two of you the chance to properly address your feelings face-to-face. Due to this breakthrough, I think it wise to start to wind down our sessions. You are both communicating with each other more openly and have made significant progress. You are back together again, which was the ultimate goal of couple's therapy. We just now need to ensure that the reconnection will be permanent. The next session we have will be in four weeks time and it

155

will be another open communication session. The focus will be where the two of you are in your relationship away from the counselling. Have things improved? Are things still the same?"

OPEN COMMUNICATION TRANSCRIPT
Session Three with Dr L Foster

DR FOSTER

Well, it's nice to see you again, Mark and Jennifer. It's been over a month now since I last saw the both of you, and when we last met, I was pleased to learn that you'd made excellent progress. So, how are things for you?

MARK

They're better than they have ever been.

JENNIFER

I agree. It's been heaven. We've really opened up to each other and we've been really close.

DR FOSTER

I take it that you're back living at home now, Mark?

MARK

Yes. After the dinner that Jen treated me to we had a really long talk about things and covered most of the issues that we wanted to get off our chests. I told her about how insecure I had felt during the time after my accident and how my off-the-scale behaviour had been hard to accept as I had no memory of it. I also brought up how hard it is for me to open up all of the time. I don't keep silent because I want to; it's because I don't know how to begin opening up. I just end up getting angry and it all just comes out in a bad way.

JENNIFER

I covered all the things that I wanted to say. I brought up my insecurities about being overlooked and therefore feeling unwanted. I also addressed my ignorance about Mark's feelings and how I should've spoke up sooner and faced the problems head on, rather than try to run away and hope that things would return to normal by themselves. I do feel closer to Mark now because now he's told me how he finds it hard to open up made it easier for me to accept that I need to approach things differently on an emotional level.

DR FOSTER

Well, you've both made excellent progress in the sessions, and the journals that you have provided throughout the course have definitely played their part in your reconciliation.

MARK

I'm glad that part's over. I'm sorry, Doc, but I hadn't been a student for a long time and I was never good at writing anyway. Writing solidly, pen in hand, for two hours or more, meant nothing to me unless I was completing a company balance sheet.

DR FOSTER

That's quite alright. Most people do find it hard to put their feelings down on paper. But did you find that it helped you both?

MARK

With me, it absolutely helped. I'm sometimes quite guarded with my emotions and I found that having to bare my soul to a blank page made the situation feel as though I was confessing a little bit to a stranger...

JENNIFER

He's definitely more open now.

MARK

To begin with, writing in the journal made me feel as though I was being put on trial to account for my feelings. I was very hesitant and didn't want to do it. But after doing it the first few times, I ended up imagining that I had already announced everything to the world, so I had no fear in speaking up again.

DR FOSTER

Jennifer, what about you?

JENNIFER

The journals were like being back at home and I was writing my diaries all over again. It was a definite learning experience, because doing something like that makes you realise that sometimes your point of view has more than one side to it. There was also that feeling of, how Mark said, this was going out into the universe and that made me feel a little bit on show with everything.

DR FOSTER

How did you arrive at those conclusions?

JENNIFER

I re-read some of the entries that I made after our last open session. Reading it allowed me to start seeing Mark's point of view a bit better in relation to my own, and helped me realise that this marriage needs both of us to make it work. I wanted Mark to prove to me that he believed in our marriage and that I was at the forefront of everything in his mind. But you don't think selflessly in that situation and going over the entries again with a fresh eye made me think to myself that maybe it would be best to just shut my mouth and listen to Mark, rather than listen to myself all of the time.

MARK

The problem was that we were both rocked by what happened on the site and in all honesty we've kept coming back to a television show that we barely knew anything about and it's brought us together.

DR FOSTER

What was it about *The Avengers* that called out to the two of you?

MARK

For me, it was because the tape that I originally saw came from my parent's home. This show was something that my parents watched, and there are times when you find yourself being open-minded about what your parents were into and what they're about as people. Putting that aside, hearing from Jen and everyone else that I was acting out parts from this show like I was a child in the playground still grabs me. I don't have any memory of doing it but everyone told me that I did. And that was how I looked into getting my marriage problems back on track. I just thought that if *The Avengers* caused a rift then *The Avengers* can fix it. I don't know if there was something in my subconscious that was influenced by the show, but it was interesting to hear that I was acting things out from it. I've secretly watched the show since and I have to say that it is good. There are elements that I would definitely bring into my home, especially the way that Steed dresses, because he always looks smart. But the other-world style of the show has only started appealing to me now and I think this is the case because *The Avengers* has had such an impact on bringing me and Jen back from the brink.

JENNIFER

With me it was completely different. Yes, the show dominated a fair few weeks of my life due to its effects on Mark and my reaction to his outlandish behaviour. But the show was an inspiration to me in the end rather than being a problem, because I remembered that Mark had told me where he got the idea for the dinner in the field from. And it was purely by chance that I found another video of *The Avengers* in that shop.

The episodes on that tape presented to me the kernel of the idea that I eventually went with. In all honesty, I have to say that I also watched the episodes that had been recorded from the True Entertainment channel as well, because they gave me the inspiration to go all out on costume, so that I could pick out outfits that were not the same but similar to those I'd seen on screen. Add that to knowing the way Mark thinks about my body and I soon had a winning combination. *The Avengers* was a big help to me...

I used it as my inspiration and it worked. I don't really understand how this show, at the time not important to either of us, could split up and then save our marriage more than once, but I'm glad that I wasn't too judgemental about it and let it work its magic on Mark and me. I think it's a cracking show. It's not one that I would watch religiously, but I think that it would help me out again if I was stuck for a surprise for Mark in the future!

(Jennifer laughs, as does Dr Foster.)

MARK
You did use it for another surprise.

JENNIFER
Oh yes, I did, didn't I?

DR FOSTER
What surprise was this?

MARK
Jen kind of got sentimental over the fact that we were nearing the anniversary of the accident. I wasn't in a mood to mark it in any way but she had an idea that we could capture something on *The Avengers* as a little bit of a nod to what helped us and brought us back together as well as tear us apart.

161

JENNIFER

I had a friend who was into video production and photography and she had a studio that was nearby. I went out with her for coffee because she was aware of all the troubles that Mark and I were having and wanted to see how things were. We then formed a plan to do something with *The Avengers*. We were unsure exactly what we could do so I left it up to her to decide.

DR FOSTER

Good thinking.

JENNIFER

Then, roughly two weeks later, I got a call from her to say that the stage was set and the costumes were ready. She didn't tell me what was going on until we got to her studio.

MARK

It's a good job I didn't know because I would've run off in the opposite direction!

JENNIFER

Yes, we had both kind of knocked the costume idea on the head, but then when we saw what she had in mind we both went for it.

MARK

It was a good idea.

DR FOSTER

What did you both do?

JENNIFER

We re-staged the opening credits to one of the colour series of *The Avengers*. What series was it, babe?

MARK
The Emma Peel one. Number five, I think it was in all.

JENNIFER
Yeah, so we dressed up in the costumes and re-enacted the thing. I wore this very comfortable yellow outfit while Mark dressed in a suit, complete with bowler.

MARK
I felt cool and odd at the same time, particularly carrying the umbrella on my arm because the first thing that you say to yourself is, "We're indoors and it's not raining, yet I need to carry an umbrella?"

JENNIFER
You looked good.

MARK
Patrick Macnee looked better.

JENNIFER
So, we filmed it all and made the special effect of me shooting the cork out from the champagne bottle and then filling the glasses before we clinked them.

MARK
I remember studying the scene before we did anything.

DR FOSTER
Extra research, Mark?

MARK
No, I just wanted to make sure that I was copying the man in the correct way. Patrick Macnee had the look of a gentleman. I don't think he even had to act that because he already was one. So, I really had to focus on his movements and get them exact because we were doing something that

163

was specifically *Avengers* related and wasn't just a builder and an accountant playing dress-up.

JENNIFER
I think we can wait for the Oscar, though!

DR FOSTER
So, what happened after filming?

JENNIFER
We got the DVD sent to us.

MARK
It was a laugh to watch.

JENNIFER
And the whole thing was set to music from start to finish. It wasn't very long but as the champagne glasses were toasted together there was a little message that appeared which read; "*The Avengers* took a lot from us but gave us so much more back." We were so happy to see that message flash up on screen because it spoke the truth about the incredible, often heartbreaking events of the past year, which had somehow been remedied so positively, all due to this old, very special TV series.

DR FOSTER
A small thank you to the people behind *The Avengers* then!

MARK
I'd give them more than just a thank you. The show has saved our marriage.

JENNIFER
Who'd have thought it possible for a TV show to save a marriage!

DR FOSTER

So, what lies ahead for you both now? How are things going in your relationship?

MARK

We're a lot closer, I think?

JENNIFER

Oh, definitely. We're both taking every day as if it's the first and we're being more thoughtful to each other. It's almost like we've had the chance to go through the wedding again and not bother with the crap that's happened.

MARK

I agree.

DR FOSTER

So where are you going from here?

MARK

Aren't you meant to tell us?

(This was a tongue-in-cheek comment from Mark.)

DR FOSTER

Well, from my side of things, the progress made has been such that I will put the case under review. This means that if things are still the way they are now after an agreed period of time, then the case is closed and we've solved your problems.

(For the benefit of the notes, Mark and Jennifer exchanged glances.)

JENNIFER

I think that we can safely say that things are fine with us now.

MARK

We're not sure if we should say anything yet…

DR FOSTER

About what?

JENNIFER

I'm pregnant. The doctors have told me that I'm nearly six weeks gone.

DR FOSTER

Oh, congratulations! That's wonderful news.

JENNIFER

Thank you.

DR FOSTER

Well, I think that can conclude this session. I'll be in touch in regards to further appointments, but in the meantime I suggest that you enjoy being expectant parents.

MARK

I'm just happy that I don't have to write any more journals. I'm nervous enough about being a father, let alone having to write about it.

JENNIFER

Unless he had a remote control for the telly in his hand, he didn't want to know. Now I've told him that I'm pregnant he's developed a nesting instinct around the house. The whole place is spotless. I think he cleans it every five minutes.

MARK

I'm nervous. Doc, do you think *The Avengers* did an episode about being an expectant father?

DR FOSTER
If they did, I think the episode was never aired! Take care, both of you.

END OF OPEN COMMUNICATION SESSION.

DOCTOR'S REPORT:
"This case has been a fascinating one from beginning to end. From the outset, Mark showed some very closed off emotions and he was only able to open up about them after being made uncomfortable within his environment. Once his shell was broken he was like a book and was brutally honest about his feelings. Meanwhile, Jennifer was living the fairytale romance that became marriage and had it rocked by an accident that she thought would never happen to her new husband. Due to the erratic nature of his behaviour, she learned about her own judgements in regards to her husband and through trial and error managed to lose those judgements and be accepting of her own faults in the process. As a couple, Mark and Jennifer seem to enjoy great physical attraction and are drawn to each other like magnets. Through coming to couple's therapy they have both realised and understood that physical attraction cannot form the only basis for marriage. There has to be emotional support and stability and they have found this through trial and error, with very pleasing results. The Gardiners are a lovely couple. Their course has been successful."

Dr Louise Foster
Couple's Therapist

CASE CLOSED

ABOUT THE AUTHOR

Roy Bettridge has been involved in the creative arts from a young age. He has been performing in stage shows since primary school and writing since the age of 15. He has gained a BTEC in performing arts in 2006 and has also studied at the University of Bedfordshire. Amongst his writing successes are a published review for rock star Sting in 2003, his first book *Look (Stop Me If You've Heard This One...) But There Was This TV Show* – inspired by his passion for the 1960s TV show *The Avengers* – a chapter in the *Avengerworld* anthology and his original novel *Flood*. He currently resides in Kettering. This is his third published book.

A JOURNEY OF REDISCOVERY THAT LEADS TO THE AVENGERS...

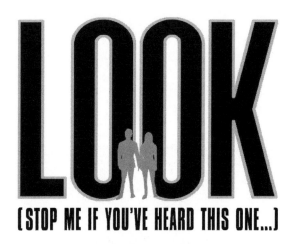

LOOK

(STOP ME IF YOU'VE HEARD THIS ONE...)

BUT THERE WAS THIS TV SHOW

ROY BETTRIDGE

Available from Lulu.com and Amazon
in print and electronic editions

JACK DRAKE TAKES A STAND AGAINST HIS TOWN, THE AUTHORITIES... AND THE WEATHER!

ROY BETTRIDGE

FLOOD

THE AVENGERS: AGENTS EXTRAORDINARY...
ITS FANS: WRITERS EXTRAORDINARY!

AVENGER WORLD

Includes an essay by author Roy Bettridge

www.hiddentigerbooks.co.uk

STEED AND KEEL ENTER THE AVENGERWORLD.
FOLLOW THEIR FOOTSTEPS IN...

TWO AGAINST THE UNDERWORLD

THE COLLECTED UNAUTHORISED GUIDE TO THE AVENGERS SERIES 1

www.hiddentigerbooks.co.uk

KEEP 'EM PEELED FOR

DR BRENT'S
CASEBOOK

AN UNAUTHORISED GUIDE TO
POLICE SURGEON

27092462R00096

Printed in Great Britain
by Amazon